D1520969

Preface

The Toby Dunbar series is a story of survival, resilience, and redemption. It is a raw, unfiltered look at the complexities of human nature and the cycles of violence, betrayal, and forgiveness that shape so many lives. Set against the harsh backdrop of the Chicago Projects and the unforgiving reality of prison life, Toby's journey explores what it means to confront fear, endure loss, and ultimately discover the strength to rise above.

Toby Dunbar is not a hero in the traditional sense. He is flawed, conflicted, and shaped by his environment in ways that challenge his sense of morality and identity. But it is precisely this humanity, this struggle to reconcile the darkness around him with the light he desperately seeks, that makes his story so compelling. Whether it's his battle to protect his life-long friend Rick's memory, his confrontations with predators like Rex "The Wolf," or his quiet moments of reflection on the choices that define him, Toby's journey is one that speaks to the resilience of the human spirit.

This series is not just about survival, it is about transformation. It is about finding hope in the darkest places, breaking free from cycles of violence, and learning to carry the weight of grief and guilt without letting it crush you. It is about the power of redemption, the importance of loyalty, and the courage it takes to live authentically in a world that often demands otherwise.

The Toby Dunbar Series is a deeply personal story, rooted in the realities of urban life but universal in its themes of perseverance and growth. It is for anyone who has faced hardship, questioned their place in the world, or searched for meaning in the face of adversity. Toby's journey is proof that even in the most unforgiving circumstances, there is always a chance for change, a chance to rise above.

Welcome to the world of Toby Dunbar. His story is one of strength, humanity, and the enduring hope that we can all find a better path forward.

Tyrone Wilson

Toby Dunbar

This book is a work of fiction. Names, characters, places and events are either products of the author's imagination or used fictitiously. Any resemblance to actual persons, living or dead, or real events is purely coincidental.

ISBN: 9798308447344

Printed in the United States of America

First Edition: 02/2025

For inquiries or more information, contact:

Email: info@tobydunbar.com

Website: www.tobydunbar.com

Tyrone Wilson

Table of Contents

Introduction

Toby Dunbar's story is one of resilience forged in the unforgiving crucible of the Chicago Projects. Growing up surrounded by poverty, crime, and broken promises, Toby learned early that survival required both strength and cunning. But it wasn't just the harsh environment that shaped him, it was the people. From family and friends to enemies and tormentors, the relationships in Toby's life revealed hard truths about loyalty, betrayal, and the delicate balance of trust.

. Toby's journey is marked by defining moments that pushed him to his limits. A childhood marred by violence and humiliation taught him to navigate fear while protecting his dignity. In the chaos of prison, Toby faced a different kind of challenge, one that tested his morality, his alliances, and his resolve to stay true to himself in a world where justice rarely prevailed. Whether confronting predators like Rex "The Wolf," enduring loss, or wrestling with guilt and rage, Toby's story is a testament to the human spirit's ability to endure, adapt, and rise above.

This book chronicles Toby's evolution, not just as a survivor but as a man seeking meaning in a world that often seemed intent on breaking him. It's a journey of self-discovery, redemption, and the unrelenting pursuit of peace.

Chapter One: Mr. Sparrow "The Terrible"

Toby Dunbar's reflections on Mr. Sparrow, a figure from his childhood, are not simple reminiscences but raw confrontations with trauma and lessons in resilience. Mr. Sparrow was a man whose cruelty left a lasting impression on Toby and others around him. At Mr. Sparrow's memorial service, sparsely attended and devoid of warmth, Toby is struck by the emptiness of the occasion, a stark contrast to the fear and control Mr. Sparrow had wielded in life.

Mr. Sparrow's life was a tapestry of cruelty and abuse, interwoven with the vulnerability of those he harmed. His wife, Mrs. Sparrow, was a kind but bed-ridden woman who relied on Toby's help. Her quiet suffering stood in stark contrast to Mr. Sparrow's unrelenting violence. Memories of Mr. Sparrow forcing Toby into dangerous situations and leaving him to fend for himself vividly remind Toby of the pivotal lessons he learned, chief among them, the importance of fighting back.

To Toby, it is not just about the terror Mr. Sparrow inspired but also about a journey of growth, self-reliance, and the determination to never let fear dictate his actions. Mr. Sparrow may have been a towering figure in Toby's past, but his lessons helped shape Toby into a man who could face adversity with courage.

A Memorial Without Meaning

Toby sat in the dimly lit dining room of the neighborhood church, surrounded by no more than ten people, each sitting in scattered chairs. The air was heavy, not with grief, but with an emptiness that spoke volumes about the man being memorialized. A single stand bore a picture of Mr. Sparrow, his expression as stern and unkind as Toby remembered. No flowers adorned the room, no heartfelt tributes echoed through the space. It was a gathering not to celebrate a life, but to acknowledge its end.

When the officiant opened the floor for remarks, an awkward silence fell over the room. The attendees exchanged uneasy glances, avoiding eye contact with the picture. Toby could feel the weight of unspoken thoughts hanging in the air. No one moved to speak; no one wanted to risk saying the wrong thing or revealing too much about what they truly felt. Eventually, the officiant thanked everyone for coming and closed the service without a single eulogy.

As Toby left the church, he reflected on the stark contrast between Mr. Sparrow's presence in life and the indifference of his passing. In life, Mr. Sparrow had loomed large, a figure of control and intimidation. His absence, however, seemed to bring relief rather than sorrow. The sparse attendance and lack of tributes underscored a truth Toby could not ignore: Mr. Sparrow had left behind not a legacy of love, but a trail of fear and pain.

Toby thought of Mrs. Sparrow, the bedridden woman who had endured Mr. Sparrow's cruelty in silence. He wondered how much of her suffering had been hidden behind closed doors, just as Mr. Sparrow's true nature had been masked by his outward demeanor. As Toby walked away from the church, he realized that Mr. Sparrow's life, though powerful in its own way, had left no lasting impact of kindness or connection, only lessons about the kind of person Toby never wanted to become.

Mrs. Sparrow: A Quiet Suffering

Toby's memories of Mrs. Sparrow were as vivid as they were haunting. Bedridden with polio, she spent her days confined to a single room, rarely venturing out even into her wheelchair. Despite her circumstances, she exuded a quiet strength that Toby could never forget. She relied on him for small tasks, like fetching her Sunday Sun Times or helping with errands, always compensating him with a warm smile and ten cents, an amount that felt generous to Toby at the time.

Mrs. Sparrow's kindness stood in stark contrast to her husband's cruelty. She had a way of making Toby feel seen and valued, even in small gestures. Yet, behind her gentle demeanor, there was an undeniable sorrow, one that spoke of a life spent enduring the harshness of Mr. Sparrow. Toby would often catch a glimpse of this sadness when she thought no one was watching, a fleeting moment where her strength wavered, and the weight of her reality became visible.

The dynamic in the Mr. Sparrow household was one of imbalance and oppression. Mr. Sparrow had moved another woman into their apartment even before Mrs. Sparrow passed away, a blatant display of disrespect that further highlighted his disregard for anyone but himself. Toby remembered how Mrs. Sparrow never complained aloud about her situation, but her silence was a loud testament to her suffering. She bore her pain with dignity, even as her world crumbled around her.

For Toby, Mrs. Sparrow represented resilience in its purest form. Her life was a stark reminder that kindness could exist even in the most oppressive environments.

Yet, her suffering also left Toby with an unsettling awareness of how easily people could be trapped by their circumstances, unable to escape the cruelty of others. Her quiet endurance became a lesson for Toby, one that taught him to recognize and reject the patterns of abuse he saw in Mr. Sparrow.

Through Mrs. Sparrow, Toby learned the importance of compassion and the strength it takes to hold onto one's humanity in the face of adversity. Her memory remained with him, a beacon of both inspiration and caution as he navigated his own struggles and sought to live a life free from the shadows of fear and cruelty.

The Early Strikes of Violence

Toby's first encounter with Mr. Sparrow's temper was both sudden and jarring. Eight-year-old Toby had been running an errand for Mrs. Sparrow, bringing her a glass of water after she called for him from her bed. Just as he placed the glass on the nightstand, Mr. Sparrow burst into the room. Without warning, he slapped Toby hard across the back of his head, sending him to the floor.

"Get the hell out of here!" Mr. Sparrow yelled, towering over Toby as if the child had committed some grave offense. Toby scrambled to his feet, tears streaming down his face, and darted out of the apartment. Before he left, he glanced back at Mrs. Sparrow, whose expression was a heartbreaking mix of shock, sorrow, and helplessness. Her lips quivered as though she wanted to speak, but no words came.

This incident marked a pivotal moment for Toby. It was the first time he experienced the raw and unprovoked violence of an adult who wielded power without accountability. The slap wasn't just physical; it was an introduction to the stark realities of unchecked authority and the vulnerability of those too small or powerless to fight back.

For days after, Toby avoided going near Mr. Sparrow's apartment. The memory of the slap haunted him, not just because of the pain, but because of the overwhelming sense of injustice it left behind. How could someone like Mr. Sparrow, who already held so much control, choose to inflict harm on someone so defenseless?

The moment also planted a seed of awareness in Toby. He began to notice how Mr. Sparrow's temper manifested in other ways, shouting at Mrs. Sparrow, manipulating his children, and ensuring that everyone around him walked on eggshells. This first strike of violence wasn't an isolated incident; it was a glimpse into the larger pattern of dominance and cruelty that defined Mr. Sparrow's interactions.

For Toby, this lesson came early but stayed with him for life: power, when unchecked, could destroy. It fueled his determination to never let himself or others be subjected to such treatment again, igniting a quiet resolve to fight back against injustice, no matter the odds.

A Family Divided

Mr. Sparrow's cruelty extended beyond individuals, it fractured his family at its core. Long before Mrs. Sparrow's passing, Toby witnessed one of the most blatant displays of Mr. Sparrow's disregard: he moved another woman into their shared apartment while Mrs. Sparrow was still alive. The shock of this action rippled through the household, leaving an already fragile family even more splintered.

Mrs. Sparrow, bedridden and physically dependent, endured the humiliation in silence. She never spoke out against Mr. Sparrow's decision, but the anguish was written across her face. Toby often saw her staring blankly at the ceiling, her hands gripping the blanket as if it were the only thing tethering her to reality. The presence of the other woman, who moved about the apartment freely and without shame, was a constant reminder of Mr. Sparrow's utter disregard for his wife's dignity.

The children, too, bore the brunt of this chaos. Jimmy and Dennis, Mr. Sparrow's sons, grew quieter and more withdrawn, their once, playful demeanor replaced by a sullen acceptance of their father's behavior. Their older sister, already grappling with her own struggles, avoided the apartment as much as possible, leaving Mrs. Sparrow with fewer allies in her corner.

Toby, an outsider who frequently ran errands for Mrs. Sparrow, felt the tension in every corner of the apartment. The other woman treated Toby with indifference, as if he were invisible, while Mr. Sparrow barked orders and enforced his dominance. For Toby, the apartment became a symbol of everything broken, a place where love and respect had been replaced by control and neglect.

This period left an indelible mark on Toby's understanding of family and loyalty. He saw how unchecked power could dismantle even the most fundamental bonds and how silence, whether from fear or exhaustion, could allow cruelty to fester. It was a lesson Toby carried with him: the importance of standing up for what is right, even when it feels impossible. Through the cracks in Mr. Sparrow's household, Toby found a resolve to build relationships founded on respect and empathy, vowing never to perpetuate the cycles of harm he had witnessed.

Chapter Two: A Cruel Test of Courage

Mr. Sparrow's capacity for cruelty knew no bounds, and it extended beyond his family to Toby as well. The most searing example of this came one fateful afternoon when Mr. Sparrow asked Toby to accompany him and his two sons, Jimmy and Dennis, on an errand. That errand led them to a poolhall in a strange neighborhood, an ominous location where Toby had no desire to visit.

The pool hall was an old wooden building with a set of concrete stairs leading into a square pit outside. A group of boys loitered there, wrestling and yelling at people as they passed by. Toby felt uneased the moment they arrived. As they entered the poolhall, Mr. Sparrow spoke briefly with someone at the counter before turning to the children. "Go outside and play," his tone leaving no room for negotiation.

Toby hesitated. "Mr. Sparrow, I don't want to go outside," he stammered, fear rising in his chest. Before he could say another word, Mr. Sparrow's fury exploded. "Boy, get out of here!" he thundered, his voice echoing off the walls. Toby had no choice but to comply.

The moment Toby stepped into the pit; he was met with hostility. One of the boys, Jake, homed in on him immediately, egged on by a ringleader named Zero. "Yeah! Beat his ass, Jake!" Zero shouted, laughing as the group closed in. Toby tried to back away, but there was nowhere to run, the concrete walls and taunting boys trapped him.

Jake lunged, his fists flying as he pummeled Toby mercilessly. The beating felt endless, each punch a reminder of how alone and powerless Toby was in that moment. Blood was running from his nose, mouth, and eye as the group finally relented, their laughter ringing in his ears.

When Toby staggered back into the pool hall, battered and shaken, Mr. Sparrow barely acknowledged him. "Sit down over there," Mr. Sparrow muttered, not even sparing Toby a glance as he chalked his pool stick. Meanwhile, Mr. Sparrow bought cheeseburgers and sodas for Jimmy and Dennis, leaving Toby hungry, humiliated, and trembling in his chair.

That day marked a turning point for Toby. The experience was a cruel test of courage, one that left him scarred but resolute. In the aftermath, he vowed never to be so helpless again. It didn't matter how big the opponent was, how many there were, or how afraid he felt; Toby resolved to fight back, even if it meant losing.

The pool hall incident became a defining memory, not because of Mr. Sparrow's indifference, but because of the lesson Toby took from it. Courage, he learned, wasn't the absence of fear, it was the determination to act in spite of it. From that day forward, Toby carried that lesson with him, using it as a shield against the challenges and injustices that would come his way.

Lessons in Fear and Strength

The poolhall beating lingered in Toby's mind like a wound that refused to heal. For days, he relived the fear, the humiliation, and the sound of the boys' laughter echoing in his ears. Yet, amid the pain, Toby began to process a deeper truth: fear was inevitable, but courage lay in the decision to act despite it.

As he reflected, Toby realized that the beating wasn't just a random act of cruelty; it was a harsh lesson in the dynamics of power and survival. Mr. Sparrow's indifference had taught him that he couldn't rely on others to protect him, not even the adults who were supposed to care. If he wanted to survive in a world where people like Mr. Sparrow thrived, he would have to learn to stand up for himself.

Fear had gripped Toby in that pit, freezing him in place and leaving him vulnerable to Jake's fists. But what haunted him most wasn't the physical pain; it was the knowledge that he hadn't fought back. "I let them beat me," Toby thought, his fists clenching in frustration. He promised himself that if he ever faced such a situation again, he wouldn't back down, no matter how terrified he felt.

This realization marked the beginning of a shift in Toby's mindset. He started paying closer attention to the people around him, observing how they navigated conflict and asserted themselves. He noticed the quiet confidence of Milton, who never seemed to back down, even when faced with tougher opponents. Milton's resilience became a source of inspiration for Toby, showing him that strength wasn't about being the biggest or the loudest, it was about refusing to be broken.

Toby also began to redefine his understanding of courage. It wasn't about winning every fight or never feeling afraid; it was about standing up, even when the odds were against him. He practiced this in small ways, speaking up when someone tried to push him around, holding his ground when others expected him to back away. Each act of defiance, no matter how small, became a building block for the strength he was determined to cultivate.

The poolhall incident remained a painful memory, but it also became a turning point. Toby learned that fear didn't have to control him and that the power to fight back was always within his grasp. It wasn't about proving anything to Mr. Sparrow or the boys in the pit, it was about proving to himself that he was stronger than the fear that had once held him captive.

Through these reflections, Toby began to embrace a new sense of self-respect. He couldn't erase the past, but he could use it as fuel to move forward. The lessons of fear and strength became a foundation for the person he was becoming, someone who could face adversity with courage and resilience, no matter how daunting the challenge.

The Unseen Strength of Mrs. Sparrow

As Toby reflected on his encounters with Mr. Sparrow, one figure consistently rose above the chaos: Mrs. Sparrow. In her small acts of kindness and quiet resilience, she had shown Toby a different kind of strength, one that did not rely on dominance but on endurance and humanity.

Mrs. Sparrow lived a life of unimaginable hardship, bedridden with polio and subjected to the daily cruelty of her husband. Yet, despite her circumstances, she remained kind and composed. She never lashed out, never let bitterness consume her. Instead, she treated Toby with warmth and dignity, making him feel valued in a world that often dismissed him.

Toby recalled the way Mrs. Sparrow would call him into her room with a soft voice, always asking for help politely and offering a small reward for his efforts. These gestures may have seemed trivial, but to Toby, they were monumental. In a home ruled by Mr. Sparrow's anger and control, Mrs. Sparrow's gentleness was a beacon of hope.

Her perseverance left an indelible mark on Toby. He often thought about how she managed to maintain her grace despite the humiliation and neglect she endured. She became a symbol of quiet strength, proving that even in the most oppressive circumstances, dignity could prevail.

Toby realized that Mrs. Sparrow's strength lay in her ability to resist becoming like Mr. Sparrow. She could have allowed her suffering to harden her heart, but instead, she chose compassion. This realization shaped Toby's understanding of resilience. Strength, he learned, wasn't just about fighting back, it was also about refusing to let cruelty define you.

Mrs. Sparrow's legacy stayed with Toby long after her passing. In moments of doubt, he often thought of her as a reminder that true strength comes from within. Her kindness, despite her pain, taught him that humanity could thrive even in the darkest corners. Through her example, Toby found the courage to hold onto his own values, even when the world seemed intent on breaking him.

Moving Beyond the Terrible

As Toby lay in his cell, at the Cook County Jail, staring at the ceiling and replaying the memories of Mr. Sparrow and his household, a quiet clarity began to settle over him. He realized that while Mr. Sparrow had inflicted pain and fear, the lessons Toby had drawn from those experiences had shaped him into someone stronger. Mr. Sparrow's cruelty, while devastating in the moment, had planted the seeds of resilience that now defined Toby's character.

As Toby thought of Mrs. Sparrow, he felt a renewed sense of gratitude for her example. Her strength had shown him that even in the face of relentless hardship, it was possible to hold onto one's humanity. Her resilience became a guiding principle for Toby as he looked toward the future.

In moving beyond the shadows of fear and abuse, Toby found a new sense of freedom. He understood that his past, while painful, had forged him into a person capable of enduring and thriving. With each passing day,

Toby resolved to live a life defined not by the wounds inflicted upon him, but by the strength he had built from them. Mr. Sparrow might have been "The Terrible," but Toby's resilience would ensure that his legacy was one of growth, courage, and unshakable self-worth.

At 19, Toby was a year younger and a few inches shorter than Milton. With his slender build, clean-shaven face, and short Afro, Toby often appeared younger than his age. His youthful appearance belied a mind that was constantly churning, always in search of meaning or understanding. It wasn't unusual to find Toby staring off into the distance or lying on his bunk in deep thought, his gaze fixed on something far beyond the gray walls of their cell. His friends from the Projects used to tease him for being too serious, dubbing him "the philosopher." While the name was meant as a joke, it wasn't far from the truth. Toby was a thinker, often dissecting life's complexities in a way that made him seem older than his years.

Milton, on the other hand, was Toby's opposite in many ways. Taller, with a wiry frame and a seemingly endless supply of energy, Milton had always been the more outspoken of the two. He had a sharp wit and a knack for finding humor in even the bleakest situations, a trait that had often landed him in trouble back in the Projects. Now, as Toby's cellmate, Milton's constant chatter was both a source of irritation and a strange comfort.

"Hey, Toby, you up?" Milton's voice broke the silence of the cell. He lay sprawled on the bottom bunk, his tone light and familiar.

Toby smirked, his sarcasm coming automatically. "No, Milton, I'm still asleep."

Milton, as usual, ignored Toby's wisecrack, plowing ahead as if it hadn't been said. "Man, we have to get out of here before we turn 26. You wanna know why?"

Toby turned his head slightly, a hint of amusement in his eyes. "Why, Milton?"

Milton sat up, leaning forward with an almost conspiratorial air. "Because," he said, "it seems like whatever a person does between the ages of 17 and 26 is what they're gonna be doing for the rest of their lives."

Toby didn't respond immediately. Instead, he stared up at the cracked ceiling, letting Milton's words sink in. They felt heavy, their truth undeniable. For the first time, the humor of Milton's chatter gave way to something deeper, a stark reflection of their situation.

Toby's stomach churned as he thought about what Milton had said. What if he was right? What if these years, these choices, defined the rest of his life? He thought about the men he had seen come and go in the housing projects, men who had seemed trapped by the paths they'd taken in their youth. Would he become one of them, forever defined by this chapter of his life?

The thought unsettled him. Toby wasn't blind to the reality of his situation. He was young, yes, but he knew how quickly life could harden into a pattern. And here he was, behind bars, sharing a cell with Milton, while the world outside kept moving forward without him.

"Man, you're too quiet," Milton said, breaking the silence again. "What, did I say something too deep for you?"

Toby managed a small smile but didn't take the bait. "Just thinking," he said, his voice soft.

Milton leaned back, his usual grin returning. "You think too much. That's your problem."

Toby let the comment slide. Maybe Milton was right, but thinking was all he had in moments like this. As he lay there, staring at the ceiling, Toby made a silent vow to himself. He didn't know how, but he had to make sure that these years didn't define the rest of his life. He had to find a way to break free, not just from the cell but from the cycle that had trapped so many before him.

And yet, the weight of that task felt immense, almost impossible. Toby closed his eyes, willing himself to hold onto hope. Somewhere, deep within, he believed there was a way out. He just had to find it before time ran out.

Toby and Milton had shared much more than their current cell; they had shared a history that began in one of Chicago's sprawling public housing projects. Growing up in a place marked by struggle, resilience, and unrelenting challenges had forged a bond between the two. It was the kind of bond that came from navigating a world where opportunities felt scarce, and survival often required as much luck as it did effort.

Chapter Three: Toby's Reality Check

Toby Dunbar was in his element at the City Colleges of Chicago. As a student majoring in Accounting and Art, his days were filled with a blend of structure and creativity that seemed to perfectly balance the two halves of his personality. Accounting appealed to his practical side, his need for order and precision, while art allowed him to explore his deeper thoughts and express himself in ways words couldn't always capture.

Every morning, Toby would arrive on campus with his sketchbook tucked under one arm and a worn notebook for accounting tucked under the other. He moved through the halls with purpose, his mind constantly switching between numbers and images, formulas and compositions.

What Toby loved most about being there, though, wasn't just the coursework, it was the people. The classrooms and hallways were filled with students from all walks of life, each bringing their unique perspectives and stories. Conversations in the cafeteria or between classes often turned into impromptu debates or exchanges of ideas. Toby thrived in these moments, listening intently, asking questions, and occasionally challenging a point when he felt strongly.

He especially enjoyed connecting with people whose experiences differed from his own. There was Maria, a single mother balancing work, school, and raising two kids. There was Jamal, a former construction worker who had decided to pursue a career in finance after an injury forced him to change paths. And then there was

Elise, an aspiring graphic designer whose passion for art often mirrored Toby's own, leading to long discussions about technique, inspiration, and the artists they admired.

Toby often found himself staying late after classes, sketching in the art studio or working through accounting problems in the library. He loved the duality of his schedule, the precision of debits and credits during the day, followed by the freedom of charcoal and paint in the evening.

The art classes, in particular, felt like a homecoming. Toby could lose himself in the act of creation, whether it was shaping a piece of clay, drawing delicate portraits, or experimenting with bold colors on a canvas. His instructors often praised his work, not just for its technical skill but for the emotion it conveyed. His classmates, too, admired his ability to capture moments and moods in his art, often asking him for advice or simply watching as he worked.

Accounting, on the other hand, challenged him in ways that excited his analytical mind. There was something satisfying about the clarity and logic of balancing a ledger, the way every number had its place, and every equation led to a concrete answer. It gave him a sense of control, a feeling that even in a chaotic world, there were systems that made sense.

For Toby, the City Colleges of Chicago was more than just a stepping stone to a future career, it was a place where he could grow, explore, and find his voice. It was a space where he could build a foundation for the life he wanted, one that transcended the limitations of his past. In the classrooms, the studios, and the conversations he shared with others, Toby found not only knowledge but also a sense of belonging. And for a young man determined to forge his own path, that sense of possibility was everything. For Toby, the campus wasn't just a place of learning; it was a sanctuary, a world far removed from the challenges he faced growing up in the projects or the tension of the Cook County Jail.

The Jello Incident

The Cook County Jail had its own rhythm, a strange
blend of monotony and unexpected hilarity. The meals
were one of the few constants, served with the same
unyielding predictability as the guards' shifts. And with
those meals came the infamous warm Jello- squishy,
gelatinous, and more often than not, a little too colorful
to be entirely edible.

Today, however, it wasn't the Jello's questionable
hue that had Toby's stomach churning. It was the sight
of Cadillac, the giant southern man, sitting across from
Toby at the lunch table, his eyes gleaming with
mischief. He grabbed his cup of the hot, liquified Jello
and eyed it like it was fine wine, raising it in mock toast
before he tilted it back, gulping it down like it was the
most refreshing drink in the world.

The sound of slurping echoed around the table,
punctuated by the unintentionally comedic sight of
Cadillac's face contorting into a mixture of delight and
disgust. It was almost as bad as the Mop-Boys' sinky
mop dance, which Toby had the misfortune of

witnessing just the day before. The Mop-Boys, a ragtag group of inmates, had taken it upon themselves to entertain the masses with their ridiculous routines, but nothing could rival the sheer horror of watching Cadillac drink that Jello.

As Toby stared into his own cup, contemplating whether to risk a sip, Cadillac leaned over, his enormous frame looming closer. "What's wrong, Toby?" he asked, his voice booming yet oddly gentle.

Toby hesitated, glancing at the murky liquid that seemed to contain more than just Jello. "It's a lot of hair and dirt in my juice," He mumbled, half-hoping he wouldn't take him seriously.

Cadillac raised an eyebrow, clearly intrigued. "Let me see that!" He reached for the cup before Toby could protest, taking it in his massive hands and inspecting it as if it were a fine specimen under a microscope.

"Sure is!" he declared, a grin spreading across his face. Then, to Toby's horror, he lifted the cup to his lips and gulped it down in one swift motion. The sight of him swallowing that murky concoction was enough to make Toby's stomach flip. "Ahhh! I hope you didn't want it!" he laughed, wiping his mouth with the back of his hand.

Toby wanted to protest, to tell him that he had absolutely no desire for that cup of hair and dirt, but the bile was already rising in my throat. He simply shook my head, his face paling at the thought of what he had just consumed.

The other older inmates, who had been watching the spectacle unfold, erupted into laughter. Cadillac was their king of comedy, and his antics never failed to amuse them. "Yeah, I got dirt and hair in mine too!" one of them chimed in, holding up his own cup, and soon enough, they were all taking turns gulping down their Jello, reveling in the absurdity of it all.

"Cheers to the Jello!" another inmate shouted, raising his cup high as if he were toasting at a banquet, and the others followed suit, laughing maniacally as they drank from their cups like it was the most normal thing in the world.

Toby sat there, wide-eyed, caught somewhere between horror and amusement. It was a bizarre little family they had formed on the tier, one built on shared meals and laughter, even if that laughter was often at Toby's expense. Cadillac's outrageous sense of humor was infectious, and soon enough, Toby found himself chuckling despite his better judgment.

"C'mon, Toby! You gotta try it!" Cadillac called out, his voice booming over the laughter. "It builds character!"

Toby looked at his cup, then back at the joyful chaos around him. Maybe it was the madness of the moment, or perhaps it was the camaraderie that had sprung up in this dismal place, but Toby couldn't help but smile. "Alright, fine," Toby said, holding up his own cup in a mock toast. "To Cadillac!"

The inmates roared with laughter as Toby took a tentative sip of what was left, bracing himself for the worst. It was as terrible as he imagined, a mix of sweetness and the unmistakable taste of dirt. But as he swallowed, he felt a strange sense of belonging wash over him, a fleeting moment of unity amid the gritty reality of their lives

"See? Not so bad!" Cadillac slapping Toby on the back, his laughter booming like thunder.

In that moment, surrounded by laughter and absurdity, Toby realized that even in a place like this, there were moments of levity, moments that reminded me of the resilience of the human spirit, even if it came from gulping down a cup of dirty Jello.

The dark humor that permeates the county jail serves as a powerful lens through which Toby confronts the harsh truths of his surroundings. In a place where hope is often a distant memory and despair lingers in the air like a heavy fog, laughter emerges as an unexpected coping mechanism. The inmates' jests, while grotesque, reveal a deeper understanding of their shared plight and the brutal lessons life behind bars imparts. Each laugh and every absurd scenario is not just a moment of levity; it is a survival tactic, a way to reclaim a sense of humanity in a dehumanizing environment.

As Toby grapples with the absurdity of Cadillac's antics, such as the revolting act of enjoying a cup filled with hair and dirt, he finds himself both repulsed and strangely enlightened. This grotesque initiation into the realities of jail life forces him to reconsider his own values and aspirations. What may initially appear as mindless revelry soon becomes a profound commentary on the choices that led each inmate to this point. The laughter echoes off the cold, concrete walls, not just as a distraction, but as a stark reminder of the life lessons hidden within the filth and chaos of the jail.

In this world where every day is marked by the struggle for dignity, the absurdity of their humor serves as a mirror reflecting the desperation and resilience of those trapped within. For Toby, witnessing such moments becomes a critical turning point. He realizes that he is standing at a crossroads, faced with a pivotal choice: to embrace the chaotic humor and the twisted sense of belonging it offers, or to seek a path away from this life, one that aligns more closely with his true self.

This decision weighs heavily on him, as he understands that the laughter may provide temporary relief, but it also encapsulates the grim reality of his surroundings. The absurdity of jail life, while darkly comedic, presents a daunting question about identity and future. Will he allow the confines of this world to define him, or will he rise above it, using these experiences as catalysts for change?

Ultimately, this moment becomes a defining crossroads, shaping not only Toby's perception of life within the jail but also his aspirations for the future beyond its cold walls. The laughter may echo long after the mops have dried, but it carries with it the weight of a decision that could alter the course of his life forever. In this complex tapestry of humor and hardship, Toby Dunbar must find the strength to choose wisely, for the path he selects will resonate far beyond the confines of the Cook County Jail, leaving an indelible mark on his identity and destiny.

Chapter Four: The Ladies on the Yard

It was Toby's second week on the tier, and he was still adjusting to the rhythms and unspoken rules of this harsh, unfamiliar environment. Today, he was being taken to the yard for the first time, a routine part of life inside. But as soon as the guards called for the tier to move, the energy shifted. Inmates were rushing around, their voices sharp and urgent, shouting things that didn't make sense to Toby.

"Them bitches are crazy!" someone yelled, prompting laughter from a nearby group.

Toby furrowed his brow, unsure of what was happening. He leaned toward one of the men, hoping for some clarity. "What's going on?"

The man shot him a glance and smirked. "The ladies have gone from one to two packs of cigarettes. You better get your two packs ready!"

"What?" Toby asked, confused.

The man didn't answer. He just laughed and walked off, leaving Toby with more questions than answers.

Toby turned to Benny, an older inmate with a reputation for knowing the ins and outs of life on the tier. If anyone could explain, it would be Benny. "What's everybody talking about?" Toby asked, his voice low enough to avoid drawing attention.

Benny gave him a knowing look but didn't offer much. "You'll see," he said cryptically.

When they got to the yard, Toby began to understand. At one end of the yard, near an old, weathered shack, there was a line of inmates. Each man held two packs of cigarettes, shuffling forward in turn. The scene was surreal, almost like some kind of grim marketplace. As Toby squinted, trying to make sense of what he was seeing, the reality hit him like a punch to the gut.

Inside the shack were a handful of inmates dressed as women. Makeup smudged their faces, and their bodies were clad in makeshift outfits meant to mimic feminine clothing. They were performing sexual acts on the men in exchange for the cigarettes. The two packs Toby had heard so much about were the price of admission.

Toby's stomach churned, and he forced himself to look away. He didn't want to stare, didn't want to draw attention to himself, but he couldn't shake the image from his mind. The scene was a stark reminder of how prison stripped away layers of identity, morality, and choice. The men who lined up weren't there out of some twisted thrill, they were there because this was their reality, because prison was a place where human needs clashed against the confines of survival.

Toby didn't judge the men in line. He couldn't. Who was he to judge? The weight of his own sentence loomed over him like a shadow. If convicted, he was facing at least 20 years behind bars. Twenty years. The thought alone was enough to make his chest tighten.

He wondered, almost fearfully, where his own sense of self, his own sexuality, would be after two decades in a place like this. How much could a person endure before the walls began to reshape them? Before their identity was chipped away, piece by piece?

The line at the shack continued to move, the scene carrying on as if it were the most natural thing in the world. But to Toby, it wasn't natural. It was a grim illustration of what prison did to people. It stripped them of their dignity, tested the limits of their humanity, and forced them into choices they would have never imagined outside these walls.

Benny nudged him. "Now you know," he said quietly.

Toby nodded, swallowing the lump in his throat. He didn't say anything in response. What could he say? The yard was a different kind of battlefield, one where survival wasn't just about strength or cunning, it was about holding onto who you were, no matter how much the world around you tried to take it away.

As the men continued to line up, Toby stood to the side, watching but not really seeing anymore. His mind was elsewhere, fighting with questions he wasn't sure he wanted answers to. All he knew was that every moment here was a test, and he wasn't sure what kind of man he would be at the end of it.

Chapter Five: Boxing with Picasso

Picasso was a man who commanded both respect and fear. From the moment Toby entered the tier, Picasso made his presence known. He was a paradox, charismatic yet intimidating, articulate yet ruthless. With a physique that resembled a professional bodybuilder and the demeanor of a seasoned CEO, Picasso stood apart from the rest. He was a figure who seemed larger than life, exuding authority with every word and gesture.

Picasso had greeted Toby with an air of formal hospitality, outlining the rules of the tier like a businessman explaining the terms of a contract. Yet beneath the veneer of civility lay a sharp mind, always calculating, always strategizing. Toby couldn't help but wonder why someone so brilliant was wasting his life behind bars. Men like Picasso, Toby had come to learn, often thrived in the confined chaos of jail but struggled in the freedom of the outside world.

A Punch Thrown in Jest

The men filtering in from the yard, sweat-soaked and restless. The atmosphere was charged with the usual mix of tension and boredom. Preston, one of the inmates with a mischievous streak, decided to shake things up. Spotting Toby leaning against the wall near the common area, Preston began throwing lighthearted jabs in his direction, grinning from ear to ear.

"Come on, Toby! Show me what you got!" Preston teased, weaving his fists in exaggerated arcs.

Toby, initially hesitant, decided to play along. "Alright, man. You asked for it," he said, throwing a couple of quick, clean jabs. His fists snapped through the air with surprising speed and precision, catching Preston off guard.

"Whoa!" Preston exclaimed, stumbling back, a mixture of surprise and laughter on his face. "Man, you can box!"

The small crowd that had gathered laughed and clapped, turning what could have been a tense interaction into a moment of camaraderie. Toby thought nothing of it, retreating to his cell to resume reading a dog-eared novel he'd borrowed from the library. To him, it was just a harmless moment of levity in an otherwise grim existence.

An hour later, as Toby flipped the pages of his book, Milton burst into the cell, his face alight with excitement and trouble.

"Toby, Picasso wants to see you," Milton announced, leaning casually against the doorframe.

Toby looked up, instantly wary. "For what?" he asked, his brow furrowing.

Milton smirked, clearly enjoying the brewing drama. "He heard you can box."

Toby's heart sank. Picasso was not the kind of man you wanted interested in you. "Milton, what did you say to him?"

Milton shrugged, feigning innocence. "I might've mentioned that you've got some moves. Relax, it's not a big deal."

"Not a big deal?" Toby said, pressing a hand to his forehead. "Milton, I'm not boxing him!"

Milton chuckled, his voice dripping with sarcasm. "Come on, his punches won't hurt any more than anybody else's."

"Well, if you're so confident, why don't you box him?" Toby shot back.

Milton grinned, unbothered by Toby's frustration. "I would, but he asked for you."

Toby sighed, already regretting the playful exchange with Preston. Picasso's interest was rarely benign, and Toby knew this was about more than just a boxing match.

By the time night fell, Toby lay in his bunk, staring at the ceiling, his thoughts a storm of anticipation and dread. This wasn't just a punch thrown in jest anymore, it was the opening move in a high-stakes game of power and survival.

The King of the Tier

The tier was its own world, a self-contained society where strength, cunning, and reputation dictated the pecking order. At the top of this hierarchy stood Picasso, the undisputed king. Every movement he made seemed deliberate, every word carefully chosen to reinforce his position. He didn't need to shout to command respect; his presence alone was enough to make the most hardened men fall silent.

Picasso was an enigma. Physically, he was a force to be reckoned with. His towering frame and chiseled physique made him look more like a professional athlete than an inmate. But it was his mind that set him apart. He spoke with a polished cadence that reminded Toby of his college professors, a stark contrast to the slang and bravado that filled the air of the tier. He had an almost supernatural ability to read people, to see through their facades and exploit their weaknesses.

Toby had observed Picasso since his first day on the tier. Unlike most who tried to dominate through brute force or fear, Picasso operated like a businessman. He introduced himself to Toby not with threats but with a handshake and a list of rules. "Hello, young man. I'm Picasso," he had said, his tone calm and measured. Then, like a CEO outlining company policies, he explained the expectations of the tier: no theft, no unnecessary fights, and absolute loyalty to his authority.

At first, Toby was taken aback by Picasso's demeanor. In a place where chaos often reigned, Picasso brought a strange sense of order. But the more Toby watched him, the more he saw the contradictions in Picasso's life. He was brilliant, charismatic, and capable of so much more than what prison walls could contain. Yet, here he was, seemingly resigned to a life of confinement. Toby wondered what had brought him to this point, what decisions or circumstances had led such a capable man to squander his potential.

Despite Picasso's intellect and composure, there was an undercurrent of volatility in him. It was like standing near a sleeping lion, you couldn't help but feel the danger even in its stillness. Toby had seen flashes of this side of Picasso, moments when his carefully controlled exterior gave way to something primal. Those moments were a stark reminder that Picasso's civility was not to be mistaken for weakness.

It was against this backdrop of authority and enigma that Picasso announced the boxing match. The dayroom was alive with its usual noise, conversations, card games, and the hum of daily routines, when Picasso's voice cut through the air.

"Toby!" he called out, his voice carrying a tone that was both commanding and casual. "I heard you can box. Be ready tomorrow."

The room fell silent. All eyes turned to Toby, who froze under the weight of Picasso's gaze. There was no malice in Picasso's expression, just a faint smile that seemed to say he already knew how this would play out.

Then, without waiting for a response, Picasso turned and walked away, his entourage following like shadows.

Toby's stomach churned. This was no ordinary challenge. Picasso didn't waste his time on frivolity, and Toby knew this wasn't just about boxing. It was a test, a way for Picasso to size him up and determine his place in the unspoken order of the tier. Toby's chest tightened. He knew what Picasso was doing, psychological warfare. The match could have happened immediately, but Picasso wanted Toby to stew in his thoughts, to overthink, to feel the weight of his gaze.

As the day wore on, Toby found himself increasingly on edge. The casual confidence with which Picaso had issued the challenge only heightened Toby's unease. Was this a simple show of dominance? A prelude to something more sinister? Or was it, as Toby suspected, part of a larger game that only Picasso fully understood?

That night, Toby sat on his bunk, replaying the day's events in his mind. He couldn't shake the feeling that this was about more than just him. Picasso's every move seemed calculated, as though he were playing chess while everyone else was stuck on checkers. Toby didn't know what the next move would be, but one thing was clear: he was now a piece on Picasso's chessboard, and the game was just beginning. He thought about the encounter with Blue, and how deception, betrayal, and calculated chess moves defined their relationship.

A Friendship Built on Quicksand

Blue, like Picasso, intellect and manipulative prowess were undeniable, a fact Toby had to reluctantly accept to finally gain the upper hand. The journey to overcoming Blue wasn't about proving superior intelligence; it was about understanding the battlefield and recognizing Blue's tactics for what they were, personal, calculated, and relentlessly destructive. For Toby, the battle went beyond chess; it was about reclaiming his autonomy and defeating a man who'd undermined his relationships, finances, and peace of mind.

Blue's actions highlighted a bitter truth: sometimes, the people closest to you can be your greatest adversaries. From sowing seeds of mistrust to outright theft, Blue's schemes showcased a level of cunning that kept Toby perpetually off balance. But when Toby began to view Blue not as a friend but as an opponent in a larger game, the dynamics shifted. By learning to think beyond the obvious and embracing strategies of deception, Toby found a way to counter Blue's moves. In the end, it wasn't about being smarter; it was about playing smarter. This incident is a testament to resilience, strategy, and the power of accepting an opponent's strengths to ultimately outmaneuver them.

From the moment Toby met Blue, there was an unspoken dynamic that drew them together. Blue's charm and confidence made him an attractive figure in the Projects, a natural leader with a sharp mind and quick wit. Toby admired Blue's intellect, often seeking his advice and trusting his judgment. However, cracks in their relationship began to show early on. Blue's need for control and his subtle manipulation of those around him were red flags that Toby initially ignored.

Blue had a way of making Toby feel indebted to him, always framing his actions as being for Toby's benefit. Whether it was warning Toby about imagined threats or stepping into situations uninvited, Blue positioned himself as indispensable. "Hey man, I didn't like the way so-and-so was looking at your mom," he'd say, planting seeds of doubt and mistrust. These "helpful" interventions often led to Toby distancing himself from others, leaving Blue as his primary confidant.

Despite the growing unease, Toby found it hard to remove himself. Blue's charm masked his true intentions, and his intelligence made him a formidable presence. Over time, Toby began to see the patterns: Blue wasn't helping him; he was isolating him. The friendship was a one-sided game, with Blue always positioning himself as the winner. The realization that their bond was built on manipulation set the stage for the conflict that would define their relationship.

The Shadow Lurking

Blue's manipulative tendencies began to show themselves in full force as he sowed seeds of distrust among Toby's friends and family. It started subtly, offhand comments about someone's intentions or loyalty, but the effects were devastating. Toby's girlfriend, Sandy, became a frequent target of Blue's whispered suspicions. "I saw Sandy talking to some guy earlier," Blue would say, "and they looked pretty close." These insinuations gnawed at Toby, even though he trusted Sandy deeply. Over time, doubts crept in, not just about Sandy but about others in Toby's life.

Blue's tactics didn't stop with Sandy. He made Toby suspicious of long-time friends, framing their actions as betrayals or signs of disrespect. "Did you hear what so-and-so said about you?" Blue would ask, his tone heavy with implication. Toby, caught between his own instincts and Blue's relentless narrative, began to withdraw from people who genuinely cared about him. Friendships that had taken years to build were dismantled in weeks, leaving Toby increasingly isolated.

Even Sandy, who was one of Toby's strongest supporters, started to feel the strain. Blue's constant interference created rifts between her and Toby, leading to arguments that hadn't existed before. Blue's goal was clear: to make himself the sole voice Toby listened to, the only person Toby trusted. And for a time, he succeeded. Toby found himself questioning everyone except Blue, unaware that the real threat was the man he had allowed so deeply into his life. This was a dark period for Toby, where Blue's schemes cast a shadow over every relationship Toby valued. The emotional toll of this manipulation would eventually drive Toby to reevaluate everything, but not before significant damage was done.

Realization and Acceptance

The breaking point for Toby came during an emotionally charged conversation with Sandy. One evening, she confronted him about Blue's comments, specifically about Toby's inability to beat him in chess. "I heard Blue telling people you couldn't beat him. He even said you read chess books and still lose. He said he conned you out of the $1200 that you had been saving all year." Sandy said, her voice tinged with both disbelief and concern. She looked up at Toby with unwavering faith. "Is that true? I don't believe it!" For Toby, this moment was excruciating. Admitting the truth to Sandy, that Blue was, indeed, smarter than him, felt like a personal defeat. And how he allowed Blue to manipulate him into thinking he had misplaced his $1200 savings. It wasn't just about chess; it was about acknowledging Blue's dominance in their lives. "Yes, it's true," Toby admitted, his voice barely above a whisper. "He's a lot smarter than me."

This vulnerability, however, was a turning point. Sandy's reaction surprised him. Rather than judging him, she offered clarity. "He's not smarter than you, Toby. He's playing YOU, not the chess pieces. He knows how you think and uses it against you. I bet he talks constantly during your games, distracting you. He's not outsmarting you; he's manipulating you."

Sandy's insight planted a seed in Toby's mind. For the first time, he began to view Blue's actions through a strategic lens. Blue wasn't unbeatable; he was simply exploiting Toby's trust and predictability. This realization marked the beginning of a shift. Toby decided to stop playing Blue's game and start analyzing his every move. By acknowledging Blue's strengths, Toby empowered himself to adapt and outmaneuver him. Toby's awakening was an acceptance of his own vulnerabilities and a resolve to turn them into strengths. It was no longer about matching Blue's intelligence but about redefining the terms of their conflict.

The Chess Match Beyond the Board

Toby's next step was to approach Blue's manipulative patterns as a chessboard where every move required precision. He began observing Blue closely, not just in their chess games but in daily interactions. Toby realized Blue's strength lay in his ability to read people and exploit their weaknesses. This wasn't about intellect in the traditional sense; it was psychological warfare.

Sandy's earlier observations became a guiding principle for Toby. He started focusing less on the game pieces and more on the person sitting across from him. During their next chess match, Toby noticed how Blue constantly talked, diverting attention from the board. "He's playing me, not the game," Toby thought. This understanding shifted Toby's strategy. He stopped responding to Blue's comments, maintaining a stoic silence that unsettled Blue.

Outside of chess, Toby applied the same approach. He began testing Blue's reactions in subtle ways, introducing small distractions or moments of unpredictability. Blue, who thrived on control, found himself momentarily thrown off balance. Each interaction became a calculated move in Toby's broader plan.

Toby also studied Blue's history. He recalled past incidents where Blue had manipulated others and identified patterns. Whether it was planting seeds of doubt or feigning vulnerability, Blue relied on the same tactics repeatedly. This analysis gave Toby the blueprint he needed to counter Blue effectively. He realized that defeating Blue wasn't about outsmarting him intellectually; it was about dismantling his psychological control.

By treating every interaction as part of a larger game, Toby started to see Blue's weaknesses. His overconfidence and need for dominance left him vulnerable to subtle, calculated moves. For Toby, this wasn't just a chess match anymore; it was a battle for autonomy, fought with patience, observation, and strategy.

The Plan Takes Shape

The realization that defeating Blue required Blue's own methods turned Toby into a strategist. He began collaborating with Milton to craft a plan that mirrored Blue's style of manipulation. Milton's advice was simple but effective: "You have to make him think he's still in control until it's too late."

The first step in their plan was to create a scenario where Toby would expose himself. Knowing Blue's habit of boasting, Toby arranged for the perfect bait: money. He left clues suggesting he would be carrying cash, deliberately using the same currency exchange that Blue often used. Milton's role was to be a bystander, strategically placed to witness any confrontation.

Toby rehearsed his demeanor, practicing the same psychological tactics Blue had used against him. He made deliberate eye contact and chose words that hinted at vulnerability, knowing Blue would pounce. "I'm just trying to keep my head above water," Toby mentioned to Blue days before their planned encounter. It was enough to convince Blue that Toby was weakening.

The pivotal moment came when Toby pretended to have lost track of his "hidden" money while in Blue's presence. Blue, as predicted, couldn't resist taking advantage. He moved in, confident that he was one step ahead. Unbeknownst to him, Milton had been observing everything from a distance. Meanwhile, Toby had planted the seeds for the next phase of his plan, ensuring Blue's arrogance would lead him to overplay his hand.

The genius of the strategy lay in its simplicity: Blue believed he had Toby cornered, but in reality, Toby was three steps ahead. Every decision Blue made, every move he thought was in his favor, had been anticipated. The stage was set for the confrontation that would finally level the playing field.

The Turning Point

The culmination of Toby's plan came at the currency exchange, where he and Milton had meticulously set the stage. Toby arrived with a backpack containing a few inconspicuous items: keys, a beeper, and a chess book.

To anyone else, it was an ordinary day, but to Blue, it was a golden opportunity. The bait had been perfectly laid, and Blue, true to form, couldn't resist taking it.

As Blue left the currency exchange, Milton intercepted him outside. "Hey, have you seen Toby? Did you take his money?" He looks different today, like he's ready to hurt somebody. He's got a gun on him. Real quiet, like he's not himself," Milton said, planting the idea that Toby suspected Blue of taking his money. Blue, always ready to take control, saw this as his moment to strike.

About an hour later Blue saw Toby going down the walkway along the field. Toby, walking a few paces ahead, kept his movements slow and deliberate. His silence was calculated, designed to unsettle Blue. When Blue caught up, he wasted no time: "Here's $900, Toby." Toby, with a deliberate puzzled look on his face, "What's this?" "Sorry Toby, I should've told you that I took it. Let's head to my place for the rest." The suggestion was laced with confidence, as if Blue were still in control. Toby agreed without argument, following Blue to his rowhouse, staying slightly behind to maintain the illusion of intimidation. Blue nervously says, "I told you that I was sorry. Why are you walking behind me like that? What's up?" "Just keep walking." Toby said, cutting Blue off.

By the time they reached Blue's rowhouse, police officers, tipped off by Blue earlier, were already positioned nearby. The final act of Toby's plan unfolded as Blue, grinning smugly, tried to manipulate the situation further. "He's got a gun! And my money's in his backpack!" Blue shouted to the police as they approached, with guns out.

What Blue didn't know was that Toby's backpack contained none of those things. As they walked, Toby subtly discarded the real bait, the cash, into nearby bushes where Milton was waiting. The police, after a thorough search, found only the mundane items Toby had packed. The smug grin on Blue's face faded into shock and humiliation as the officers turned their attention to him. Toby, calm and composed, couldn't suppress a small, victorious smirk.

Though Toby was taken in for questioning, the absence of evidence against him made it clear he'd outmaneuvered Blue. The look of betrayal and disbelief on Blue's face was the ultimate checkmate, a moment that symbolized Toby's triumph over years of manipulation and control.

Winning the War, Not the Battle

Reflecting on his tumultuous history with Blue, Toby began to see his conflicts in a new light. For years, he had tried to match Blue's intellect and outmaneuver him in direct confrontations, always coming up short. Blue's manipulative prowess and sharp mind had made him a formidable opponent. But now, looking back, Toby realized that it wasn't Blue's intelligence that had been his greatest challenge, it was his own inability to think strategically beyond the moment.

Toby had learned that winning wasn't always about outsmarting someone in every move; it was about using the resources and knowledge available to him to shift the balance in his favor. His final encounter with Blue was proof of this. By setting the stage carefully, leveraging advice from others like Milton, and executing a calculated plan, Toby had managed to turn the tables on someone who had controlled the narrative for years.

The lessons were clear. First, never underestimate the value of patience and observation. Toby's ability to watch and learn from Blue's patterns had been key to dismantling his psychological control. Second, the importance of relying on a support system became evident. People like Milton and Sandy had provided insights and encouragement that Toby couldn't have found on his own. Lastly, Toby learned to detach from the need to prove himself to Bue. True victory lay not in defeating Blue outright but in reclaiming his peace and autonomy.

Toby's journey with Blue wasn't about proving who was smarter. It was about rising above a toxic dynamic that had weighed him down for years. In the end, Toby emerged with a renewed sense of clarity and strength. He understood that while Blue might always pride himself on his intellect, Toby had gained something far more valuable, the ability to choose his battles and define success on his own terms.

Chapter Six: The Boxing Match

The dayroom was unusually quiet the next day, the air thick with anticipation. Everyone knew what was about to happen, and all eyes were on Toby. As he made his way across the room, he felt the weight of their stares, each one a silent question: Would he stand his ground, or would Picasso break him?

Picasso entered with his entourage, his presence bringing the usual hum of activity to a halt. Dressed in a white tank top that accentuated his muscular frame, he looked more like a heavyweight champion than an inmate. He carried himself with an air of casual confidence, his every step radiating control. When he reached the center of the room, he turned to Toby with a slight nod and a faint smile.

"You ready, Toby?" Picasso asked, his tone calm but charged with expectation.

Toby's heart pounded in his chest. He didn't feel ready, not by a long shot, but he couldn't afford to show weakness. Taking a deep breath, he nodded. "Yeah, I'm ready."

The crowd formed a loose circle around them, the tension palpable. Picasso's reputation loomed large, and everyone expected him to dominate. Toby wasn't just fighting Picasso; he was fighting the perception of being an easy target.

Without warning, Picasso threw the first punch. BAM! The impact sent Toby stumbling backward, his arms barely able to block the blow. The force of it felt like a battering ram, and Toby's mind reeled. Before he could recover, Picasso pressed forward, weaving and throwing air punches with terrifying speed and precision.

"Get up!" Picasso barked, his voice cutting through the cheers of the onlookers.

Toby scrambled to his feet, his body already aching. He realized Picasso wasn't just strong, he was relentless. But Toby wasn't about to roll over. Gritting his teeth, he stepped forward and countered with two quick jabs and a right cross. The punches connected, surprising both Picasso and the crowd.

The dayroom erupted with shouts and cheers. Toby could feel a surge of adrenaline as he saw a flicker of acknowledgment in Picasso's eyes. But the moment was short-lived. Picasso retaliated with a devastating blow to Toby's side. CRACK! Pain shot through Toby's ribs, and for a moment, he thought they might be broken.

Milton's words echoed in Toby's mind: "His punches won't hurt any more than anybody else's." He wanted to laugh at the absurdity of it. Picasso's punches felt like they were designed to break bones, not just land points.

As Picasso came in for another strike, Toby saw his chance. Timing it perfectly, he delivered a powerful uppercut just as Picasso ducked. POW! The punch connected squarely with Picasso's mouth. Blood spattered across the floor, and the room went silent.

Picasso staggered back, raising a hand to his face. "How bad is it?" he asked one of his crew.

"It's bad, man. You need to get that looked at," someone replied.

Picasso's bottom lip was split open, a gruesome gash that exposed the raw flesh underneath. Despite the injury, Picasso seemed unfazed. He stuffed a t-shirt into his mouth to stem the bleeding and turned back to Toby.

"Let's finish," Picasso said, his voice muffled by the blood-soaked fabric.

Toby's stomach churned. The sight of Picasso, still ready to fight with blood dripping down his face, was like something out of a nightmare. He could see the madness in Picasso's eyes, the kind of unrelenting determination that couldn't be reasoned with.

As the fight continued, Toby found himself on the defensive, more focused on avoiding Picasso's wild swings than landing punches of his own. His arms felt like lead, and every movement sent waves of pain through his battered body. He wasn't just fighting Picasso's strength, he was fighting the mental exhaustion of facing someone who seemed unstoppable.

The fight only stopped when a lookout shouted, "Guard's coming!" The room scattered in seconds, inmates retreating to their cells like cockroaches fleeing the light.

Picasso, still clutching the t-shirt to his mouth, leaned in close to Toby. "We'll talk about this later," he said, his voice low and deliberate.

Toby's legs felt like jelly as he watched Picasso walk away. He knew the fight wasn't over, not really. The physical battle had ended, but the psychological game was just beginning. Picasso's injury might have been a temporary victory, but the look in his eyes made one thing clear: Toby had crossed a line, and there would be consequences.

That night, lying on his bunk, Toby stared at the ceiling, every muscle in his body aching. He replayed the fight in his mind, analyzing every punch, every move, every word. He didn't just feel like he'd fought a man, he felt like he'd stepped into a world of games and strategies where every action had a price. And Toby knew that with Picasso, the price was always steep.

The Cost of Victory

The cell block was eerily quiet that night, but Toby's mind was anything but. He lay flat on his bunk, staring at the cracked ceiling, his body aching from the brutal match with Picasso. The fight replayed in his mind like a film stuck on a loop: the power of Picasso's punches, the roar of the crowd, the sickening crack of flesh and bone, and the moment his fist split Picasso's lip open. He had won a momentary victory, but it didn't feel like triumph, it felt like stepping into quicksand.

Toby knew the rules of this place. Nothing came without consequence, especially not an injury to someone like Picasso. The scar on Picasso's lip wasn't just a physical mark; it was a symbol, a reminder of the moment Toby had defied the king of the tier. In a world where reputation was everything, Picasso's injury meant more than pain, it meant a dent in his power.

A week passed, but the shadow of that fight lingered. Picasso's crew had started following Toby wherever he went, their presence subtle but unmistakable. Whether he was on the yard, the showers, or the dayroom, they were always there, watching, waiting. It wasn't overt aggression, but it was enough to set Toby's nerves on edge. He felt like a mouse under the watchful eyes of circling hawks.

Picasso, for his part, seemed to relish the tension. He didn't need to say much to remind Toby of what had happened. All it took was a knowing smirk, a subtle touch to his scar, or a quiet comment spoken just loud enough for Toby to hear.

"This thing's permanent, you know," Picasso said one afternoon, tracing a finger along his lip as he leaned against the railing of the tier. "You're going to owe me for this, Toby."

The way he said it sent a chill down Toby's spine. It wasn't an outright threat, it was something worse. It was a promise.

Toby tried to stay focused, to block out the noise and keep his head down. But the constant pressure was getting to him. He started sleeping less, his nights spent staring into the darkness, anticipating the moment Picasso would make his move. The fight had proven he could stand up to Picasso physically, but this was a different kind of battle, one fought with psychological tactics and subtle power plays.

Milton noticed the change in Toby's demeanor. "You're wound up tighter than a clock, man," he said one night as they sat in their cell.

Toby shook his head. "You don't get it. This isn't over. He's playing with me."

Milton chuckled, his usual bravado on full display. "Yeah, he's playing with you, but that's all it is. You showed him you're not a pushover. That's gotta count for something."

Toby didn't respond. He appreciated Milton's optimism, but he knew better. Picasso wasn't the kind of man to let things go. If anything, Toby's defiance had only made him more determined to assert his dominance.

The tension came to a head one afternoon when Toby was in the dayroom, trying to lose himself in a book. Picasso's crew filed in, one by one, taking seats around the room. It wasn't unusual for them to hang out in the dayroom, but their deliberate positioning made it clear they weren't there to relax.

Picasso arrived a few minutes later, his movements as smooth and calculated as ever. He didn't look at Toby right away, instead engaging in light conversation with one of his men. Then, without warning, he turned and locked eyes with Toby.

"You've been quiet lately," Picasso said, his voice carrying just enough volume to cut through the low hum of conversation. "I hope you're not avoiding me."

Toby forced himself to meet Picasso's gaze. "Not avoiding you. Just staying out of trouble."

Picasso smiled, but it didn't reach his eyes. "Good. Trouble has a way of finding people, though. Wouldn't want you to think you're off the hook."

The comment hung in the air, heavy with unspoken meaning. Toby knew it was another move in Picasso's game, another reminder that he was being watched.

That night, as Toby lay in his bunk, he couldn't shake the feeling that the fight with Picasso had been only the beginning. The scar on Picasso's lip might fade over time, but the tension between them wouldn't. Toby had stepped into a game he hadn't asked to play, and the stakes were higher than he could have imagined.

The cost of victory, Toby realized, wasn't just the pain in his ribs or the sleepless nights. It was the constant weight of uncertainty, the knowledge that every interaction, every word, every glance was part of a larger battle for control. And in this world, control was everything.

The Confrontation

It started with a warning. Benny, one of the more observant inmates, appeared at the cell door, his expression serious. "Picasso's coming for you," he said, his voice low but urgent.

Toby's pulse quickened. He wasn't surprised, he had been waiting for this moment since the fight, but hearing it confirmed sent a chill down his spine. He glanced at Milton, who was already reaching for the two shanks hidden beneath the mattress.

Milton handed one to Toby, the sharpened piece of metal cold and unforgiving in his hand. "Just keep your back to the bars," Milton said, his voice steady. "I'll be right outside."

Toby nodded, gripping the shank tightly. It felt crude and dangerous, the kind of weapon that didn't belong in anyone's hands.

The cell felt smaller than ever, the walls closing in as Toby positioned himself near the back, his body tense but outwardly calm. He knew Picasso was smart, smart enough to spot any sign of fear or hesitation. If he showed weakness now, it could cost him everything.

The sound of footsteps echoed down the tier, each one heavy with purpose. Picasso's crew arrived first, one of them entered the cell like a shadow. He positioned himself against the wall, by Toby, another by the doorway, their faces unreadable but their presence menacing. Then Picasso stepped in, his movements deliberate and controlled. He stopped near the end of the bunk, just far enough to keep an exit open but close enough to loom over Toby like a storm cloud.

"Evening, Toby," Picasso said, his voice calm, almost conversational.

Toby forced himself to maintain eye contact. "Evening," he replied, his tone neutral.

The air in the cell was thick with tension, the kind that made every second feel like an eternity. Toby's mind raced, analyzing every detail, the positioning of Picasso's men, the distance between them, the weight of the shank in his hand. And the sharp edges biting into his palm, and he couldn't tell if the moisture he felt was sweat or blood.

He had set it up so that Picasso's henchman was closest to him, pinning the man against the wall and leaving Picasso with a clear path to retreat. Toby knew he wasn't as strong or cunning as Picasso, but in this confined space, he didn't have to be.

"How are we going to fix this?" Picasso asked, gesturing vaguely to his lip.

Toby didn't respond immediately. He could feel his heart pounding in his chest, but he kept his expression steady. He was waiting, ready for the moment things might turn violent.

Picasso stepped closer, his presence almost suffocating. "This is a permanent scar, Toby. I need to be compensated."

Toby gripped the shank tighter, his body coiled like a spring. He didn't trust Picasso, not for a second. Every word, every gesture felt like part of a calculated performance designed to lower Toby's guard.

Before Toby could make a move, Picasso's expression shifted. His lips curved into a slow, unsettling grin, and he let out a deep, booming laugh. It wasn't the laugh of someone who had let go of a grudge, it was the laugh of someone who had been in control all along.

"What did you think I wanted, Toby?" Picasso asked, his voice tinged with amusement.

"Relax, Toby," Picasso had said, leaning casually against the bunk as his crew chuckled. "You thought I wanted booty?

Toby kept his face neutral, his grip on the hidden shank loosening slightly but not enough to let it go. "What do you want, Picasso?"

Picasso's smile widened, his scarred lip twisting into an expression that was both amused and calculating. "It's simple," he said, gesturing to his face. "This scar? It's permanent. A parting gift from you. So, I figure it's only right you give me something in return."

The sudden change in tone was disorienting, but Toby didn't lower his guard. He watched as Picasso leaned casually against the bunk, his scarred lip twisting into a smirk.

"I want you to draw my portrait," Picasso said, surprising Toby. "And I want a Dutch apple pie from commissary every week. That's all."

The tension in the room broke as Picasso's crew started laughing, the sound echoing off the cell walls. Even Milton, standing just outside, let out a small chuckle. But Toby didn't join in. He knew better.

This wasn't just a demand for a portrait or pie. It was a test, a way for Picasso to remind Toby, and everyone else, that he still held the upper hand. Toby had passed the physical challenge in the dayroom, but this was something deeper. It was a way to see if Toby could be intimidated, manipulated, or drawn into a web of obligation.

Toby nodded, keeping his tone measured. "Alright, I'll draw it. And the pie?" Picasso smiled, his eyes glinting with satisfaction. "Good man."

After laying out his demands in the cell, Picasso's booming laughter had echoed through the tier, catching everyone off guard. It wasn't the laugh of a man who had forgiven or forgotten. It was a laugh laced with confidence, a laugh that said, 'I'm still in control, and don't you ever forget it.'

The words hung in the air, their weight more significant than the casual tone in which they were delivered. Toby stayed silent, waiting for the rest.

"I want a portrait," Picasso continued, his eyes narrowing slightly. "You've got talent, I've seen your sketches. Draw me. Something good. Something that'll make me look as sharp as I am. And" he paused, letting the moment stretch before delivering the kicker "I want a Dutch apple pie from commissary. Every week."

"A pie?" Toby asked, his voice steady but cautious.

Picasso tilted his head, his smile taking on a mischievous edge. "Yeah, a pie. Call it my sweet tooth. And a little reminder that we've got an understanding."

Toby forced himself to nod. "Alright. The portrait and the pie. That's it?"

"For now," Picasso said, his grin never wavering. "See, I'm not unreasonable, Toby. I don't take more than what's fair. You've got my word on that."

But it wasn't Picasso's words that lingered with Toby, it was the way he delivered them. The smile, the laughter, the camaraderie he tried to build in those moments all felt calculated. It was clear to Toby that Picasso's requests weren't just about a scar or a sweet tooth. This was about power, about testing Toby's loyalty and willingness to comply.

As Picasso and his crew filed out of the cell, Toby let out a slow, controlled breath. The confrontation hadn't turned violent, but it had revealed the depths of Picasso's control. He wasn't just a man of brute strength; he was a master of psychological warfare, capable of bending others to his will with a mix of charm and intimidation.

Later, Toby sat on his bunk, the shank still hidden under his pillow. He had survived the confrontation, but he knew the game was far from over. Picasso's demands might seem small, but they were a foothold, a way to keep Toby within his sphere of influence. And in a place like this, even small debts had a way of growing into chains.

A Villain's Smile

The confrontation in the cell had left Toby rattled, but what followed was even more unnerving. Picasso had a way of turning the tides of tension, taking moments that seemed poised to erupt into violence and transforming them into something else entirely, something no less dangerous, but disarmingly calm.

That night, as Toby sketched out rough outlines for Picasso's portrait in the dim light of his cell, he replayed the interaction over and over in his mind. Picasso had defused the tension in a way that made him seem magnanimous, almost charming, but Toby wasn't fooled. The portrait and the pies were just symbols, tokens of submission. Agreeing to the terms felt like stepping into quicksand, easy enough at first, but impossible to escape once you were in too deep.

Milton leaned back on the bunk above, breaking the silence. "You got off easy, man. A picture and some pie? Could've been worse."

Toby didn't respond immediately, his pencil scratching against the paper. "It's not about the pie," he finally said.

Milton peered down at him. "Then what's it about?"

"It's about seeing if I'll bend," Toby said, setting the pencil down and looking at the rough sketch. "If I say yes to this, what's next? He's not asking for much now, but he's making sure I know he's in charge."

Milton shrugged. "You gotta pick your battles, Toby. Sometimes it's easier to play along."

Toby nodded, but his instincts told him otherwise. He'd agreed to Picasso's terms because refusing would have escalated things, but he couldn't shake the feeling that this was just the beginning. Picasso didn't do anything without a reason, and Toby knew better than to assume the demands would end here.

As the tier quieted for the night, Toby stared at the half-finished portrait. It was good, a sharp likeness of Picasso's strong features and commanding presence, but there was something unsettling about capturing a man like him on paper. It felt too much like acknowledging his power, like giving him something he could use as a trophy of control.

Toby set the drawing aside and lay back on his bunk, his thoughts racing. Picasso had smiled and laughed, but Toby recognized the villain's smile for what it was: a

mask, a warning, and a reminder that no one on the tier
was truly free.

Chapter Seven: The Rules of Survival

Jail had its own set of rules, a code unwritten but universally understood. Toby had learned them quickly. In a world where metal bars and cement walls defined the physical boundaries, it was the invisible boundaries, the ones shaped by power, intimidation, and manipulation that truly dictated survival.

The first rule Toby had come to understand was that strength wasn't always about muscle. It was about perception. The strongest man wasn't necessarily the one who could win a fight but the one who could make others believe he was untouchable. Picasso embodied this principle perfectly. He didn't need to remind people of his authority with violence, his presence alone was enough.

Toby reflected on his own position in this hierarchy. The fight with Picasso had changed things. While it had earned him a measure of respect, it had also placed him in a precarious spot. He wasn't just another inmate anymore; he was the guy who had dared to land a punch on the king of the tier. That kind of attention was dangerous.

Picasso's crew had begun to watch Toby more closely, their movements subtle but intentional. They weren't overtly hostile, but their presence was a constant reminder that Picasso's eye was always on him. Toby understood the message: he might have passed one test, but there would always be another.

Milton, ever the opportunist, seemed to take the situation in stride. "You've got their attention now," he said one evening, lounging on the top bunk with his usual nonchalance. "That's not a bad thing, you know. Means they respect you."

"Respect isn't free," Toby replied, leaning against the wall. "It comes with strings."

Milton grinned. "Yeah, but better to have respect with strings than no respect at all. You've seen what happens to guys who don't have it."

Toby didn't need the reminder. He had witnessed the consequences of being perceived as weak or vulnerable. Those were the men who became targets, who were used and discarded like pawns in someone else's game.

But Toby wasn't content to play someone else's game. Every instinct told him that his survival depended on maintaining his autonomy, his dignity, and his sense of self. Picasso's demands, the portrait, the pies, were small in the grand scheme of things, but Toby saw them for what they were: an attempt to chip away at his independence.

As the days passed, Toby began to study the dynamics of the tier more closely. He watched how Picasso's crew interacted with each other and with the other inmates.

They moved like a pack, each member playing a specific role. There was the enforcer, the one who made sure debts were paid. The lookout, always scanning for guards. The middleman, who handled negotiations and smoothed over conflicts. Together, they formed a well-oiled machine, with Picasso at the helm.

Toby also observed Milton, whose survival strategy was entirely different. Milton was a chameleon, someone who could blend in and make himself useful to anyone in power. His charm and quick wit allowed him to navigate the delicate balance of power on the tier. Milton was a little odd at times, but Toby knew he could trust him with his life. Toby reflects on growing up with Milton. He often crossed paths with Milton at school and occasionally at Milton's house when Toby accompanied his mother on visits. They lived in the high-rise buildings of the Projects, while Milton's family occupied one of the rowhouses nearby. Although only a year older than Toby, Milton's physical stature made him seem much more mature. When they graduated from grammar school, Milton was already an imposing six feet tall, while

Toby was a modest 5'5". For Toby, Milton's height and confidence added an aura of wisdom, even if he often cloaked it in humor.

As a child, Toby always thought of adults as impossibly old, their authority unquestionable. Among the neighborhood figures who seemed to epitomize this timeless adulthood was Mr. Davis. A sturdy man in his 60s, Mr. Davis exuded a calm sense of control. Whenever he took a group of kids fishing, he would bark orders to Grady, Arkansas, and Linzy, three men in their 40s who always followed his instructions without question. To Toby, it seemed natural that Mr. Davis was in charge, though he couldn't quite put his finger on why. That was just the way of things.

Milton, however, had a knack for peeling back the surface of ordinary situations and exposing the strange truths beneath. He often had everyone in stitches with his outlandish observations and razor-sharp wit. His sense of humor drew people in, but it was his ability to blend hilarity with surprising insight that made him unforgettable.

One summer afternoon, as Toby, Milton, Rick, and a few other kids sat on the cracked concrete steps outside the rowhouses, Milton decided to reveal the "truth" about Mr. Davis. The kids were restless, the oppressive heat making everything feel heavier, the sun, the air, even their curiosity. Milton's sudden pronouncement shattered the lethargy like a dropped glass.

"Y'all wanna know why it seems like Mr. Davis is always bossing Grady, Arkansas, and Linzy around?" Milton asked, a mischievous glint in his eye.

The kids leaned in, their attention piqued by Milton's tone.

"Man, that's just 'cause he's old," Rick replied dismissively, wiping sweat from his brow.

Milton shook his head with exaggerated exasperation. "No, no, no. It's deeper than that. See, when Mr.Davis was a grown man, those three were little kids! He used to babysit them when they were knee-high!"

The group erupted into laughter, the absurdity of the idea catching them off guard. The thought of the gruff, authoritative Mr. Davis wrangling a trio of mischievous toddlers was too funny to bear. Even Toby, who admired Milton's knack for weaving comedy into conversation, laughed so hard he had to clutch his stomach.

"You're crazy, Milton!" one of the kids choked out between fits of laughter.

But Milton remained calm, his expression unwavering. "Nah, I'm serious. Think about it. When you're a kid, all the grown folks look the same age to you. But there's a big difference between being 40 and being 60. Mr. Davis probably sees them the same way he did back when they were running around in diapers."

Toby, catching his breath, considered the logic of Milton's words. While it still seemed ridiculous, there was something about the explanation that made sense. Adults weren't a monolith; they had histories, relationships, and roles that extended far beyond what kids could perceive. Maybe Mr. Davis's authority wasn't just about age but about history, shared experiences that shaped how people related to one another, even decades later.

As the laughter subsided, Milton leaned back on the steps, looking unusually contemplative. "Man, y'all gotta remember, the world doesn't start when we're born. People have their own stories, their own pasts. We're just stepping into it halfway through."

The kids didn't know how to respond to that, so they didn't. For all his jokes and wild ideas, Milton had a way of dropping truths that left everyone quiet. It was as though he could see beyond the cracks in their world, finding the invisible threads that held everything together.

For Toby, that moment lingered long after the laughter had faded. As the years went by, he often thought about Milton's words, especially when he found himself trying to understand the complicated dynamics between the adults in his life. It was the first time he had realized how much history could shape people's behavior, how the past bled into the present in ways that weren't always obvious.

Milton, with his towering height and sharp mind, became a kind of neighborhood visionary. He had a way of blending the absurd with the profound, wrapping life lessons in humor so they went down easier. And even though Toby had always thought of Milton as older and wiser, he realized that wisdom wasn't about age or stature. It was about perspective, the ability to see the bigger picture and share it with others.

Looking back, Toby saw that Milton had taught him one of his earliest lessons about humanity: that everyone, no matter how commanding they seemed, had a story shaped by those who came before them. The world wasn't divided into the powerful and the powerless, the old and the young. It was a mosaic of overlapping histories, each piece influencing the others in ways that were both subtle and profound.

In that summer heat, sitting on the concrete steps, Toby had laughed along with the rest of the kids. But deep down, he knew Milton wasn't crazy. He was wise in a way that only a few people could be, a wisdom born not of years, but of insight. And for Toby, that realization made all the difference.

Although Toby had great admiration for Milton, he wondered how much of himself Milton had given up to maintain his position in jail.

For Toby, the answer was clear. He wouldn't let anyone take his sense of self, no matter the cost. The fight with Picasso had been as much about asserting his independence as it had been about survival. Toby knew he couldn't control everything, there would always be forces beyond his power, but he could control how he responded.

Late one night, as the tier settled into its uneasy quiet, Toby sat on his bunk and pulled out the nearly finished portrait of Picasso. It was one of his best pieces, a sharp and commanding likeness that captured both Picasso's physical presence and the cunning intelligence in his eyes.

Milton leaned over to look. "That's good," he said, his voice low. "Really good. You could sell something like that on the outside."

Toby didn't respond immediately. Instead, he stared at the drawing, his pencil hovering above the paper. "It's not just a picture," he said finally. "It's a symbol. For him, it's a trophy. For me, it's a reminder."

"A reminder of what?" Milton asked.

"That I'm still me," Toby said, setting the pencil down. "And I'm not going to let anybody take that away from me."

In the days that followed, Toby carried that resolve with him. He met Picasso's gaze without flinching, spoke carefully but firmly, and made it clear through his actions that he wouldn't be anyone's pawn.

The unspoken rules of jail life were harsh, designed to strip men of their dignity and turn them into shadows of themselves. But Toby was determined to rewrite those rules for himself. He couldn't change the system, but he could refuse to let it change him.

In a place where so many had lost their sense of identity, Toby clung to his with a quiet but unyielding strength. It wasn't easy, and it wasn't without cost, but it was the only way he knew how to survive. And for Toby, survival meant more than just staying alive, it meant staying whole.

Drawing Lines

The cell was quiet except for the soft scratch of Toby's pencil against the paper. He was seated cross-legged on his bunk, the portrait of Picasso spread out in front of him. It was nearly finished, a remarkable likeness that captured not just the man's physical features but the commanding presence that defined him. Toby worked carefully, adding shading to highlight the sharp angles of Picasso's jawline and the intensity in his eyes. The process wasn't just about drawing, it was about understanding.

As the portrait took shape, Toby found himself reflecting on Picasso in ways he hadn't before. The man was undeniably powerful, but his strength wasn't just in his physique. It was in his ability to control people, to manipulate them into giving him what he wanted. Picasso was like a master chess player, always thinking three moves ahead, always positioning himself to win.

Toby's pencil paused as he studied the image. It struck him that the portrait wasn't just a representation of Picasso's face; it was a symbol of their relationship. Every stroke of the pencil felt like a dialogue, a silent conversation about power, respect, and the thin line between the two.

There was respect there, Toby couldn't deny it. Picasso's intelligence and charisma were undeniable, and in another life, under different circumstances, he might have been someone Toby admired. But there was also fear. Not the kind of fear that made Toby cower, but the kind that kept him hyper-aware of every interaction, every word, every move.

Picasso's demands, the portrait, the pie, weren't random. Toby saw that now. They were calculated, a way for Picasso to assert his dominance without resorting to outright violence. By asking Toby to draw his portrait, Picasso wasn't just testing his loyalty, he was forcing Toby to acknowledge his power, to literally put it on paper for everyone to see.

When the portrait was finally complete, Toby leaned back and studied it. It was good, better than good. The sharp contrast of light and shadow gave Picasso an almost regal appearance, his scarred lip adding a layer of complexity to his expression. There was pride in the drawing, but there was also something darker, something that made Toby's stomach twist.

Milton, who had been watching from his bunk, leaned over to get a closer look. "Damn," he said, his voice tinged with genuine admiration. "You really outdid yourself. That's him, alright."

Toby nodded, but his expression was somber. "Yeah, that's him."

Milton smirked. "He's gonna love it. You think this means he'll ease up on you?"

Toby shook his head. "This isn't about easing up. It's about reminding me who's in charge."

Milton shrugged. "Maybe. But you gotta admit, it's better than him breaking your ribs."

Toby didn't respond. He slid the portrait into a folder to protect it, his hands lingering on the edges of the paper. The drawing felt heavy in his hands, not because of its physical weight but because of what it represented.

When he finally handed the portrait to Picasso later that day, the reaction was immediate. Picasso's eyes lit up as he unrolled the paper, his expression shifting from curiosity to approval.

"This is... impressive," Picasso said, his voice carrying a tone of genuine appreciation. He held the drawing up, showing it to his crew. "See this? This is what I'm talking about. Man's got real talent."

The crew murmured their agreement, nodding and offering Toby a few approving looks. For a moment, the tension between Toby and Picasso seemed to dissipate, replaced by an odd sense of camaraderie.

But Toby wasn't fooled. As Picasso rolled the portrait and slipped it under his arm, he leaned in close, his voice low enough for only Toby to hear.

"You did good, Toby," he said, his tone almost friendly. "But remember, this isn't just a picture. It's a reminder. You and me? We've got an understanding now."

Toby nodded, keeping his expression neutral. "Yeah, we do."

As Picasso walked away, the portrait safely clutched in his hand, like a trophy, Toby felt a mix of emotions. He had fulfilled the demand, passed the test, but the cost was more than just time and effort. The portrait was a symbol of their complex relationship, a blend of respect, fear, and manipulation that left Toby walking a fine line.

That night, as Toby lay in his bunk, he thought about the lines he had drawn, both on the paper and in his life. Picasso had his portrait, his pie, and his subtle show of dominance, but Toby still had his dignity, his manhood. He had played the game on his terms, refusing to let Picasso strip away his identity or sense of self.

In the quiet darkness of the cell, Toby made a silent vow. He would keep walking that line, balancing between survival and resistance, but he wouldn't let anybody push him over the edge. In a world designed to break men, Toby was determined to hold onto the one thing no one could take: his own sense of who he was.

Chapter Eight: Locked Up with a Mystery

After nearly a year inside, Toby was beginning to feel the cracks in his own identity, the slow unraveling that came from living in a world where survival often meant suppressing your sense of self. The routine had become a blur: the harsh clang of doors, the relentless tension of life on the tier, and the ever-present question of whether he could hold onto the man he once was.

One afternoon, after a frustrating court appearance that yielded no progress on his case, the guards shuffled him into a holding cell to wait for transport back to his block. As the heavy door closed behind him, Toby froze. Sitting on the bench across the room was someone who appeared to be a woman.

For a moment, Toby's mind couldn't reconcile what he was seeing. The delicate features, the soft curves, it all pointed to one conclusion. But this was a men's jail, and he knew that the women's facility was in an entirely different building. The longer he stared, the more unsettling the experience became. Was he imagining things? Had he been in here so long that he was starting to lose his grip on reality?

He avoided eye contact, shifting uncomfortably on the bench as his thoughts spiraled. 'Is it happening to me?' he wondered, panic creeping into his chest. Toby had seen how the environment broke men down, how the confines of prison reshaped their minds and desires. The lines between need and identity blurred in a place like this, and now Toby was questioning his own.

The figure across the room adjusted their posture, catching Toby's glance for a fleeting moment. There was a calm confidence in their expression, as if they were entirely at peace with who they were, a stark contrast to the storm brewing in Toby's mind.

His thoughts raced. 'How long before I end up like some of the guys on the yard? How long before I start lining up with my two packs for the ladies in the shack?' The question terrified him. Was this what prison did? Did it strip you down so completely that you didn't recognize yourself anymore?

Toby clenched his fists, his nails digging into his palms as he tried to ground himself. He thought of Sandy, of the life he wanted to rebuild, of the dreams he still held onto. This place wasn't going to take those from him. It couldn't. But as the minutes ticked by in that holding cell, the presence of the enigmatic figure across from him continued to unsettle him, forcing him to confront fears he hadn't dared to voice.

When the guards finally came to move him, Toby felt both relieved and shaken. As the door clanged open, the figure gave him a parting glance, one that felt oddly understanding, as if they knew the questions that had been gnawing at him. Toby left the cell with a heavy heart, carrying not just the weight of his case but the realization of how deeply jail was testing his sense of self.

A Moment of Reflection

As Toby entered the cell, the familiar clang of the metal door barely registered in his mind. His thoughts were elsewhere, consumed by the surreal encounter in the holding cell earlier that day. Milton, as always, was eager for updates. From his spot on the bottom bunk, he leaned forward with an excited grin. "How did everything go in court?"

Toby stood there for a moment, still processing the day. "It was good," he finally said, his voice distant. "I might be getting out next week."

Milton's grin widened. "What? That's great news, man! You should be happy!"

But as Milton's excitement filled the small cell, Toby's lack of enthusiasm became impossible to ignore. He was staring at the wall, lost in thought, his brow furrowed.

Milton's expression shifted to confusion. "What's wrong? What happened?"

Toby hesitated, then sat down on the edge of his bunk, running a hand over his face. "On the way back, they put me in a holding cell with what appeared to be a woman... but it had to be a man."

Milton raised his eyebrows but quickly caught himself, leaning back casually. "Man, that was a test!" he said with a chuckle, trying to lighten the mood. "They're always testing people in here. You know how it is, they want to see how you react."

Toby shook his head, unconvinced. "I don't know. Maybe I've been here too long. It's messing with my head."

Milton's grin faded slightly as he looked at Toby. He could see that this wasn't just some passing concern. Toby's voice carried a weight that spoke to something deeper, a crack in the armor that Toby had worked so hard to maintain during his time behind bars.

"Listen," Milton said, his tone softer now, "this place is designed to mess with you. But you can't let it. You're almost out of here, man. Don't let this place get in your head right before you're free."

Toby sighed, leaning forward with his elbows on his knees. "I keep thinking about it. The way they sat there, calm and confident, like they knew exactly what they were doing, like they knew I wouldn't be able to look at them without questioning myself. It wasn't just them. It's this whole place. It gets into you, changes the way you see everything."

Milton nodded slowly, recognizing the gravity of what Toby was saying. "Yeah, it does," he admitted. "But that's why you gotta hold onto yourself. Hold onto what's real. Don't let this place win. You've made it this far, Toby. Don't let something like this mess with your head now."

Toby looked at Milton, appreciating the sentiment but still feeling the weight of the encounter. "I don't want to start doubting who I am," he said quietly.

"And you won't," Milton replied firmly. "You've got a life waiting for you outside these walls. Focus on that. Focus on Sandy, on school, on everything you've got going for you. You're not gonna end up like the guys who get stuck in here. You're almost there."

Toby nodded, though the unease lingered. As he lay on his bunk later that night, staring at the ceiling, he thought about Milton's words. He wanted to believe them, to hold onto the idea that he could leave this place behind without it leaving a permanent mark on him. It wasn't just about the figure in the holding cell; it was about what they represented. The experience had forced him to confront the cracks forming in his own identity, the fear that the longer he stayed in this place, the harder it would be to hold onto who he was. But as unsettling as it had been, it also strengthened his resolve. He couldn't let this place define him. No matter how long he was here, Toby promised himself, he wouldn't lose sight of the man he was, and the man he wanted to become. He was almost free, but freedom wouldn't erase the cracks that had already formed. All Toby could do was hope that once he stepped outside these walls, the pieces of himself would still fit together.

Chapter Nine: Toby's Release

Toby was counting the days until his release. After months of navigating the dangers of incarceration, he could finally see a light at the end of the tunnel. But as freedom approached, so did a looming threat: Picasso. Known for his violent past and iron grip over the tier, Picasso had spent more time locked up than free. Toby had heard the warnings from Benny and others, stay far away from Picasso. Yet avoiding someone like Picasso wasn't easy.

Toby's focus was on leaving without incident, but Picasso seemed determined to make that difficult. From cryptic comments to veiled threats, Picasso's presence was impossible to ignore. Worse, Toby feared the consequences for Milton, who would remain behind after Toby's release. As Toby prepared for his final days inside, he had to confront the fear that freedom might come at a cost, and that cost could be Milton.

The Shadow of Picasso

Toby sat on the edge of his bunk, listening carefully as Benny leaned in closer, his voice low and deliberate. Benny, a grizzled veteran of the prison system, had become something of a guide for Toby, offering advice on how to navigate the tier's unspoken rules. Today, however, Benny's words carried an edge of urgency.

"You know Picasso's been locked up most of his life, right?" Benny began, glancing over his shoulder to ensure they weren't being overheard. "The guy's a certified maniac. He got ten years for shooting two people when he was just sixteen. Then he gets out and, bam, he shoots someone else and does another ten years. Now, he's back again. Nobody knows exactly what for, but you better believe it's something crazy."

Toby nodded, but the weight of Benny's words settled heavily in his chest. Picasso's reputation was already well-known, a fact that Benny was now elaborating on with grim detail.

"Picasso isn't just violent," Benny continued. "He's smart. He's got this... way of getting into people's heads. He doesn't just throw punches; he plays chess while everyone else is playing checkers. He can make you feel like you don't have a choice, like you're walking into his trap before you even know it's there."

Toby had seen glimpses of this control. Picasso rarely raised his voice, but when he spoke, people listened. On the tier, he moved with an air of authority, his henchmen always a step behind, ready to act on his unspoken commands. He didn't need to shout or threaten; his reputation alone was enough to make most men step aside.

Benny's tone softened, but his eyes were sharp. "Listen to me, Toby. You're almost out of here. You've kept your head down, and you've got a shot at getting out clean. But Picasso? He'll try to do you in before you get out. That's how he works. If he can't have you under his thumb, he'll find a way to mess you up. So stay far away from him."

Toby nodded again, his face a mask of calm, but inside, a flicker of unease had ignited. He had worked so hard to keep a low profile, to avoid the power games that dominated life in the jail. The thought of becoming a target now, so close to freedom, filled him with a quiet dread.

The rest of the day passed with an undercurrent of tension. Toby couldn't help but watch Picasso from a distance, studying the way he interacted with others. Picasso was always composed, his movements deliberate, his words calculated. He didn't need to exert physical force; his presence alone was enough to control the room.

Benny's warning echoed in Toby's mind: "He'll try to do you in." Toby understood now that it wasn't just a possibility, it was a likelihood. Picasso wasn't the type to let things slide, especially not when it came to someone slipping beyond his reach.

That night, as Toby lay on his bunk, staring at the cracked ceiling, he made a silent vow. He would heed Benny's advice and stay as far from Picasso as possible. But in the back of his mind, he knew it might not be that simple. Picasso wasn't just a shadow on the tier, he was a storm waiting to strike. And Toby needed to be ready.

The First Confrontation

The yard was its usual chaos, a mix of clanging weights, shouted conversations, and tense undercurrents that Toby had learned to navigate carefully. He stuck to his routine, keeping to the edges and focusing on his thoughts. With his release only days away, he was doing everything he could to stay invisible, to avoid any unnecessary attention. But the tension on the tier followed him like a shadow, and today, that shadow had a name: Picasso.

Toby was mid-stride, the cool air sharp against his skin, when he heard the voice behind him. It wasn't loud, but it carried the weight of authority. "I heard you're leaving me."

Toby's heart jumped, and for a brief moment, he froze. He recognized that voice, Picasso's voice, calm, deliberate, and laced with something that felt like a veiled threat. Slowly, Toby turned to see Picasso standing a few feet away, flanked by two of his henchmen. Their expressions were unreadable, but their presence alone spoke volumes.

"Hey, what's up, Picasso?" Toby said, forcing a calmness he didn't feel.

Picasso took a step closer, his lips curling into a faint, knowing smile. "I heard you're leaving me," he repeated, as if savoring the words.

Toby felt his blood begin to boil. The way Picasso said it, possessive, almost intimate, set his nerves on edge. He knew exactly what Picasso was doing. This wasn't a casual comment or a friendly goodbye. It was a game, a way to test Toby's resolve and gauge his reaction.

"I might be released in a few," Toby said carefully, keeping his tone neutral.

Picasso tilted his head slightly, studying Toby like a predator sizing up its prey. "So, when were you going to sit down and talk to me about it?" His tone was light, almost playful, but the words carried an unsettling weight. The way he said it, as if Toby owed him something, sent a ripple of anger through Toby's chest.

Toby clenched his fists, fighting the urge to snap. Losing his temper here, in front of Picasso and his crew, would only give them more power over him. He took a slow breath and straightened his posture. "I'm a man," Toby said, his voice steady but slightly louder than normal. "I'm not your bitch, Picasso."

For a moment, time seemed to stand still. Picasso's smile faded, replaced by an unreadable expression. His henchmen shifted slightly, as if preparing for something. Toby's muscles tensed, ready for whatever might come next.

Then, unexpectedly, Picasso burst into laughter. The sound was sharp and unsettling, echoing across the yard. "Okay," Picasso said, still chuckling. "I guess Milton will have to keep me company."

The comment hit Toby like a gut punch, but he kept his face neutral, refusing to give Picasso the satisfaction of a reaction.

"Until the next time, Toby," Picasso added, his tone almost sing-song as he turned and walked away, his henchmen trailing behind him.

Toby stood there for a moment, his heart pounding as he processed what had just happened. He had held his ground, asserted his independence, but he knew Picasso's laughter wasn't the end of it. It was a warning. And the comment about Milton? That was a threat, thinly veiled but unmistakable.

As Toby walked away, his mind churned. He wasn't worried about himself; his release was close, and he could see the finish line. But Milton didn't have that same luxury. Toby knew his friend had dismissed the threat, brushing it off with his usual bravado, but Picasso wasn't the kind of man to make idle comments. Toby's chest tightened as he considered the possibilities. Could he really leave, knowing Michael might be in danger?

That night, as Toby lay in his bunk staring at the ceiling, the confrontation replayed in his mind. He had managed to keep his composure, but the encounter left him shaken. Picasso wasn't just testing him, he was leaving a mark, a reminder that his reach extended far beyond the yard. Toby's fight for independence wasn't over, and the stakes were higher than ever.

Chapter Ten: A Friend in Danger

Toby couldn't shake Picasso's words: "I guess Milton will have to keep me company." The laughter, the casual way Picasso had said it, it wasn't just a comment. It was a message. Toby had seen enough of Picasso to know that everything he did was deliberate. He didn't waste words, and when he spoke, it carried intent. The threat was clear, even if it had been cloaked in humor.

Back in the cell, Milton was lying on his bunk, flipping through an old magazine. The sight of him, relaxed and seemingly carefree, only made Toby's unease deepen.

How could Milton be so calm, so unconcerned, when Picasso's shadow was looming over them both?

"Hey," Toby said, leaning against the wall. "We need to talk about what Picasso said today."

Milton didn't look up. "What about it?"

Toby frowned, frustrated by his friend's nonchalance. "You know what about. That comment he made about you. He wasn't joking, Milton. He's planning something."

Milton finally set the magazine aside, looking up at Toby with a smirk. "Man, you're overthinking it. Picasso likes to mess with people. That's all it is, mind games."

"Mind games?" Toby said, his voice rising slightly. "Milton, this is Picasso we're talking about. He's not playing around. You know what he's capable of."

Milton shrugged, his grin unwavering. "Yeah, I know. But I'm not scared of him. I'll be fine, Toby. You're the one about to walk out of here. Focus on that."

Toby felt a surge of frustration. Milton's bravado was infuriating, but Toby knew it was a defense mechanism. It was easier for Milton to laugh it off than to acknowledge the danger. But Toby couldn't laugh it off. The thought of leaving Milton behind, vulnerable to whatever Picasso had planned, made his chest tighten with guilt.

That night, as Toby lay in his bunk, staring at the ceiling, his thoughts wouldn't stop racing. He couldn't help but replay every interaction he'd seen between Picasso and his henchmen, every whisper, every subtle glance. Picasso's power wasn't just in his physical presence; it was in his ability to manipulate, to control, to make people feel trapped even when they weren't.

Toby wanted to believe Milton's confidence, but he couldn't ignore the gnawing feeling in his gut. What if Milton wasn't as safe as he thought? What if Picasso used Toby's departure as an opportunity to tighten his grip on the tier, and Milton became collateral damage?

The internal conflict was suffocating. On one hand, Toby was so close to freedom, so close to leaving this nightmare behind. On the other, he couldn't shake the feeling that he was abandoning Milton to face Picasso alone. He had fought so hard to stay out of trouble, to avoid getting drawn into the power struggles that defined life in jail. But now, as his release loomed, it felt like the hardest decisions were still ahead of him.

Toby turned onto his side, closing his eyes in a futile attempt to block out the thoughts swirling in his mind. He had to find a way to protect Milton, even if it meant taking risks he'd worked so hard to avoid. Freedom was within reach, but it came with a price. And Toby wasn't sure if he was willing to pay it if it meant leaving his friend behind in Picasso's crosshairs.

The Last Batch

The cramped cell was filled with the faint, sour smell of fermenting fruit, a smell Toby had grown used to over the months. It wasn't glamorous, but making hooch had become a small ritual, a way to pass the time and maintain a sense of normalcy in a place where nothing felt normal. Tonight, though, it felt different. This was Toby's last batch. His release was just days away, and the significance wasn't lost on either him or Milton.

Milton sat on the bottom bunk, grinning as he watched Toby work. "Man, look at you. Toby the Hooch

Man, one last time!" he teased, laughing so hard he nearly fell off the bunk.

Toby rolled his eyes but couldn't help a small smile. "Yeah, yeah, get your laughs in. This might be the last time you see real craftsmanship in here," he shot back, his tone dry but playful.

Milton chuckled, his laughter echoing in the cell. "You're gonna leave behind a legacy, Toby. They'll be talking about your hooch for years!"

Toby shook his head, letting out a soft laugh as he carefully let the air out of the plastic bag holding the fermenting brew. The moment was lighthearted, almost normal, but beneath the surface, Toby's unease lingered. Every time he glanced at Milton, he couldn't help but think about Picasso's comment in the yard.

Milton, always perceptive, noticed the change in Toby's expression. "Alright, out with it," he said, leaning forward. "What's on your mind?"

Toby hesitated, his hands pausing mid-motion. "I just... I keep thinking about Picasso," he admitted.

"That comment he made about you. It wasn't a joke, Milton."

Milton waved a dismissive hand. "Toby, you're overthinking this. Picasso's not gonna do anything to me. He just likes to mess with people."

"That's what you keep saying," Toby said, his tone firmer now. "But we both know what he's capable of. You've seen it."

Milton shrugged, leaning back against the wall. "Look, I know you're worried. I get it. But I'm not worried about Picasso. I've been here long enough to handle myself. I'll be fine."

The confidence in Milton's voice was reassuring, but Toby wasn't convinced. He wanted to believe Milton's words, but the nagging doubt in his mind wouldn't let him. He knew Milton was trying to ease his guilt, trying to make it easier for him to leave without worrying. But the thought of leaving his friend behind, vulnerable to Picasso's manipulation, made Toby's stomach churn.

"Milton," Toby began, his voice softer now, "you don't have to pretend everything's fine for my sake. I know what kind of person Picasso is. I just don't want"

Milton cut him off with a grin. "I know what you're gonna say, and I appreciate it. But seriously, I'll be okay. You've got your own life to focus on, Toby. Don't let Picasso take that away from you."

Toby nodded, but the unease didn't leave him. He finished sealing the hooch, setting it aside for the night, and sat down on the bunk opposite Milton. The two of them talked for a while longer, reminiscing about their time together and joking about the chaos of jail life.

Despite the humor, Toby couldn't shake the weight in his chest. As the night wore on, the laughter faded, replaced by a quiet tension that neither of them addressed directly. Milton's reassurances had brought some comfort, but Toby's mind kept returning to the yard, to Picasso's laughter, and to the lingering threat he couldn't ignore.

As Toby lay on his bunk that night, staring at the ceiling, he felt torn. Freedom was so close, but the thought of leaving Milton behind gnawed at him. Picasso wasn't just a bully, he was a force of nature, and Toby knew better than to underestimate him. The question wasn't whether Picasso would act, it was when. And Toby could only hope that Milton's confidence was more than just bravado.

Chapter Eleven: Preparing for the Unknown

Toby's final days in jail were anything but peaceful. Each morning, as the tier stirred to life, Toby felt the tension in his chest tighten. Freedom was so close, but the thought of leaving without knowing what might happen to Milton weighed heavily on him. Picasso's shadow loomed over everything, his cryptic words, his unsettling laughter, and the way his henchmen always seemed to be watching.

Picasso himself kept his distance, which only made Toby more uneasy. The lack of direct confrontation felt strategic, as though Picasso were biding his time. Every encounter with his crew felt like a test, their lingering stares and smirks designed to remind Toby that Picasso's presence extended beyond their conversations.

Benny, ever the seasoned survivor, noticed Toby's unease. One afternoon, he pulled Toby aside near the tier's common area. "Listen, kid," Benny began, his voice low but firm. "You're almost out of here, and that's great. But don't get too comfortable. Picasso doesn't let people walk away that easy. You've got to stay sharp. Watch your back, keep your head down, and don't give him any reason to come after you."

Toby nodded, appreciating Benny's advice but knowing it wasn't enough. "I'm more worried about Milton," he admitted. "Picasso made it clear he's not done with him."

Benny sighed, shaking his head. "Milton's a tough guy, but he's not invincible. You can't save him from everything, Toby. The best thing you can do is get out of here and take care of yourself."

Toby didn't respond right away. Benny was right, there was only so much he could do from the inside. But Toby wasn't ready to leave Milton entirely to his fate. That evening, he sat on his bunk, sketching out ideas in his mind. He needed a plan, something to ensure Milton's safety after he was gone.

Over the next few days, Toby began quietly putting pieces into place. He spoke to Benny about keeping an eye on Milton, knowing that Benny's influence on the tier could help mitigate Picasso's reach. He also sought out a few other inmates he trusted, planting subtle reminders that Milton wasn't alone and shouldn't be left vulnerable.

At the same time, Toby maintained his distance from Picasso, avoiding direct eye contact and steering clear of his crew whenever possible. But even as he kept his head down, he could feel the unspoken threat lingering in the air. Picasso was patient, and Toby suspected he was waiting for the right moment to strike, whether at Toby or Milton.

The nights were the hardest. As Toby lay on his bunk, staring at the ceiling, his mind raced with scenarios. What if Picasso made his move before Toby's release? What if Milton's confidence wasn't enough to keep him safe? The questions swirled in his head, robbing him of sleep.

On his final night inside, Toby sat quietly with Milton, the two of them sharing a meal and a few jokes. Milton, as usual, brushed off Toby's concerns with his easygoing charm. "You're worrying too much," he said with a grin. "Picasso's not gonna do anything to me. He's all talk."

Toby forced a smile, but the unease in his chest didn't fade. He didn't want to leave with regrets, but he also knew he couldn't let fear hold him back. As much as he wanted to stay and protect Milton, he had to trust that the steps he'd taken would be enough.

The next morning, as Toby prepared to walk out of the jail, he glanced back at the tier one last time. His heart ached at the thought of leaving Milton behind, but he knew there was no turning back. Freedom was calling, but it came with a heavy burden, a burden Toby would carry with him as he stepped into the unknown.

The Final Night

The atmosphere in the cell was strangely calm, but Toby could feel the tension simmering just beneath the surface. Tomorrow, he would be free. The thought should have filled him with relief, even joy, but instead, it brought a heavy mix of anxiety and dread. He glanced at Michael, who was perched on the bottom bunk, flipping through an old magazine. For months, Milton's easygoing demeanor had been a source of comfort, but tonight, it felt like a mask, one Toby couldn't quite see through.

"Last night in here, huh?" Milton said, breaking the silence. He didn't look up from his magazine, but his tone carried a note of wistfulness.

"Yeah," Toby replied softly, sitting on the edge of the top bunk. He hesitated before continuing. "Feels... strange."

Milton tossed the magazine aside and leaned back against the wall. "Strange how? You're about to get out. That's a win, man."

Toby nodded, staring at the floor. "It's not that. It's everything. I feel like I'm leaving unfinished business. Like I'm walking away from something I should be fixing."

Milton grinned. "If you're talking about me, don't. I told you, I'll be fine. You've got your own life to focus on. Don't let this place keep a hold on you once you're out."

Toby wanted to believe him, but the unease in his chest didn't fade. "You're sure? Because I keep thinking about Picasso, what he said, what he might do. I can't just pretend everything's fine."

Milton sighed, leaning forward. "Look, Toby, Picasso's all about control. He wants you to leave here worrying about him. Don't give him that power. You've done your time. Tomorrow, you walk out of here and start fresh. Let me handle what happens in here."

The words were reassuring, but Toby could see the faint flicker of concern in Milton's eyes. It was subtle, almost imperceptible, but it was there. They both knew Picasso wasn't someone to be underestimated.

As the evening wore on, they talked about lighter things. memories from before jail, dreams of what the future might hold. Milton joked about finding a job that didn't involve making hooch or dodging guards, and Toby shared his plans to finish school and build a life with Sandy. For a little while, it felt like they were just two friends sharing hopes and dreams, the weight of their circumstances temporarily lifted.

But as the lights dimmed for the night, the tension returned. Toby lay on his bunk, staring at the ceiling, his thoughts racing. His chest felt tight, his mind running through scenarios of what Picasso might do, whether to Milton or as a parting shot at Toby before his release.

The sound of shuffling footsteps broke through Toby's thoughts, and his body tensed. He craned his neck to see the shadowy figure passing by the cell. It was Picasso. He moved slowly, deliberately, pausing just long enough for Toby to catch the faint glint of his smile in the dim light

"See you around, Toby," Picasso murmured, his voice barely audible but unmistakably threatening. Then, just as calmly as he had appeared, he continued down the tier, disappearing into the darkness.

Toby's heart pounded in his chest. Picasso's subtle appearance was no accident, it was a calculated move, a reminder that his presence would linger long after Toby walked out those doors.

As Toby lay back down, he felt a mix of fear and determination. He couldn't let Picasso's games consume him, but he couldn't ignore them either. He thought of Milton, still inside, and silently promised himself that this wouldn't be the end of their story. Tomorrow, Toby would leave this place behind, but the uncertainty of what he was leaving, and who he was leaving behind, would follow him into the outside world.

Walking Free

Toby's release day arrived with a strange mix of emotions swirling in his chest. He stood in the processing area as the guards handed him back his belongings, a small plastic bag containing the few items he'd entered with months ago. The weight of the bag felt insignificant compared to the weight of everything he'd experienced inside. His heart raced as the heavy door slid open, revealing the sunlight and freedom waiting on the other side.

As Toby stepped out into the fresh air, the warmth of the sun hit his face. He paused, taking a deep breath. For months, he had dreamed of this moment, of walking out of the jail and leaving it all behind. But now that it was here, the relief was tinged with an unexpected heaviness. He was free, but Milton wasn't.

The ride home was quiet, his thoughts louder than the hum of the car. Sandy had come to pick him up, her smile wide and her eyes shining with joy. She talked about the plans she'd made for his return, the people eager to see him, and the future they could finally start building together. Toby nodded and smiled, but his mind kept drifting back to the tier, to the faces he'd left behind, and most of all, to Milton.

That night, as Toby lay in his own bed for the first time in months, the unfamiliar comfort of it felt disorienting. He thought about Milton, still in that tiny cell, still under Picasso's shadow. The guilt gnawed at him. He had promised himself he'd do something to protect Milton, but now that he was on the outside, the question was how.

Freedom didn't feel as simple as Toby had imagined. He felt the invisible tether of his time in jail, the lessons, the fears, and the bonds he had formed there still pulling at him. Picasso's threat lingered in his mind, a dark cloud hanging over the relief of being home.

Toby began to formulate a plan. He couldn't let Picasso's games consume him, but he also couldn't ignore them. Maybe he couldn't act directly, but he could find ways to ensure Milton's safety. He'd check in regularly, speak with Benny or anyone else he could trust inside, and stay connected to what was happening on the tier. He wouldn't abandon Milton to Picasso's manipulations.

As he stared at the ceiling, Toby made a silent vow. Freedom wouldn't mean turning his back on the people who had been part of his journey. Milton had been his friend, his brother through the darkest times, and Toby wouldn't let him face those dangers alone. Whatever it took, he would protect Milton, even if it meant walking back into the shadows he had just escaped.

The night was quiet, but Toby's resolve was loud. He was free, but the fight wasn't over. It never really was. Freedom wasn't just about walking out of the jail, it was about holding onto the people and the parts of himself that mattered most. And for Toby, that meant ensuring Milton's survival, no matter the cost.

Chapter Twelve: A Shifting Shadow

After what felt like an eternity, Toby was finally released. The day he stepped out of the jail, the cold air felt sharper, the sunlight brighter, as though the world itself had shifted during his time inside. Freedom was a breath of fresh air, but it came with an uneasy weight. Toby wasn't the same person who had walked into that cell months earlier. He was more cautious, more guarded, and far more aware of how fragile freedom could be.

The Loop Gangsters

The chaos in the theater was deafening, shouts, laughter, the scrape of chairs being knocked over, and above it all, Sandy's panicked voice. "Hey, stop it! Somebody call the police! Stop it!" she screamed, her cries cutting through the commotion. Toby was on the floor, crawling between the rows of seats while blows rained down on him from all directions. Kick! Smack! Slice! The Loop Gangsters, a group of wannabe thugs, were relentless, but Toby wasn't the same person he had been when Jake had beaten him mercilessly years ago. This Toby had learned to fight back, even against impossible odds.

A Fight for Survival

The gang's numbers worked against them. There were so many of them trying to get to Toby that they got in each other's way. "Move! Wait! Beat his ass!" they shouted, jostling for space to land blows. One of the bigger guys picked Toby up off the floor, but each time he did, Toby swung with all his strength, landing punches on whoever was within reach. He wasn't fighting to win, he was fighting to survive.

The sting of a box cutter slicing the back of his neck added to the chaos. Toby felt the warm trickle of blood, but it didn't stop him. Fueled by adrenaline and rage, he crawled to the end of the aisle and finally stood up. For the first time, he was on equal footing. Swinging with all he had, Toby turned the tide.

The Gang Flees

The fight barely lasted 10 seconds after Toby got to his feet. The Loop Gangsters scattered like leaves in the wind, running out of the theater and leaving Toby bloodied but standing. Sandy rushed to his side, tears streaming down her face. "Are you alright?" she sobbed, her hands hovering as though unsure where to touch him without causing more pain. "You have to go to the hospital!"

Despite the blood dripping from his neck and the bruises blooming across his body, Toby's thoughts were elsewhere. He wasn't worried about himself; he was worried about how Mrs. May, Sandy's mother, would feel about all of this. Toby and Sandy were out celebrating his release from jail. It seemed like trouble followed him everywhere, and he hated the thought of dragging Sandy deeper into his chaotic world.

At the Hospital

The police arrived and took Toby to the hospital first. The doctor focused on the cuts on the back of his neck, cleaning and stitching them with practiced efficiency. The pain was sharp but fleeting, eclipsed by the swirling thoughts in Toby's mind. He kept replaying the fight, the moment he stood up and forced the gang to flee. There was a grim satisfaction in knowing they had run, but the weight of the whole incident still pressed heavily on him.

After the hospital, Toby was taken to the police station. He braced himself for the worst, expecting to be charged for his involvement in the fight. But then, one of the gang members spoke up, telling the police what had really happened. "He was just trying to talk with us when one of the guys pushed him over the chair. Then we all started beating him up," the guy admitted. He even revealed the name of their group, the Loop Gangsters.

The confession cleared Toby of any wrongdoing, and to his relief, he wasn't charged with anything. It felt like a blessing, but Toby chose not to press charges against the gang. They hadn't hurt Sandy, and to him, their cowardice in running away when he stood up was punishment enough. "They're bitches," he muttered to himself, feeling a mix of anger and disdain.

In that moment, Toby's mind drifted to Zero, as it always did when he found himself facing internal conflict. No matter how much he despised Zero for killing Rick, the comparison between them lingered in his thoughts like an unwelcome guest. It was a truth he didn't want to admit but couldn't ignore: deep down, in some unsettling ways, he was just like Zero.

Zero wasn't a man of empty words. For all his cruelty, there was a twisted consistency in his actions. He hated cowards, and Toby realized, to his discomfort, that he shared the same disdain. What separated them, Toby told himself, was what they did with that hatred. Zero used it as a weapon, a way to dominate and destroy. Toby, on the other hand, struggled to use it as a tool for growth, to push himself away from the weakness he once despised in himself.

Rick's Courage

Toby's thoughts turned to Rick, his life-long friend, the guy who had defied Zero's rule with unflinching courage. Rick wasn't like the rest of them, not like Toby, Milton, or any of the others who avoided Zero and his crew whenever possible. Rick had been fearless, or at least he made it seem that way. "Fuck Zero! He don't run shit here!" Rick would say with a casual confidence that inspired and terrified Toby at the same time. Rick's words weren't just bold; they were a declaration of independence, a refusal to bow to fear.

It wasn't that Rick was reckless, though it sometimes seemed that way, it was that he refused to live his life looking over his shoulder. He walked his own path, regardless of the threats Zero posed. Toby admired Rick for that, but it also filled him with guilt. He knew he had never been that brave, and perhaps that's what made Zero hate Rick so much. Guys like Zero, Picasso, and Killer Rob despised cowards, but they reserved their deepest hatred for those who stood up to them without fear, those who wouldn't play their game.

Toby's Reflection

As Toby sat there, the weight of his thoughts pressed down on him. He hated Zero for what he had done to Rick, but what sickened him most was the part of himself that saw the world through a lens similar to Zero's. Zero admired courage, even in those he destroyed, and Toby couldn't deny that he did too. But where Zero weaponized that admiration to tear others down, Toby wanted to use it to build himself up.

He thought back to his younger self, the boy who had let fear dictate his actions. He hated that version of himself, the one who cowered in the face of Jake's fists, the one who avoided confrontation instead of standing his ground. But now, he understood something he hadn't then: it was okay to feel fear when facing danger or the unknown. Fear wasn't the problem. It was what you did with that fear that defined you.

Rick had taught him that. Rick faced fear and walked through it, never letting it define who he was. Zero, for all his bravado, used fear as a weapon, projecting it onto others to hide his own insecurities. Toby was caught between the two, torn between the person he had been and the person he wanted to become.

A Turning Point

As Toby reflected on the parallels between himself and Zero, he felt a shift deep within him. He realized that acknowledging his flaws, his fear, his moments of weakness, wasn't the same as succumbing to them. He could hate what Zero stood for, but he didn't have to let that hatred consume him or define his actions. Rick had shown him that courage wasn't the absence of fear but the ability to act in spite of it.

In that moment, Toby made a quiet vow to himself. He would honor Rick's memory not by avoiding fear, but by confronting it head-on. He would use the lessons Rick had left behind to guide him, even in the face of people like Zero. Because in the end, it wasn't Zero's hate or power that mattered, it was the strength to rise above it. And Toby knew that strength was something Rick would have wanted him to find, even if it took him a lifetime.

A Celebration of Freedom

The wounds on his body were healing, but the scars of the experience lingered. As they sat together, Toby couldn't help but reflect on how close he had come to something far worse. He glanced at Sandy, her laughter filling the air, and felt a pang of guilt. No matter how much he tried, trouble seemed to find him, and Sandy always ended up caught in the crossfire.

But for now, he allowed himself to enjoy the moment. He was free, Sandy was safe, and he had stood his ground when it mattered most. The Loop Gangsters might have won the battle, but Toby had won the war, one punch, one step, one survival at a time.

Rebuilding his life became his immediate focus. He often thought about what Milton said, "it seems like whatever a person does between the ages of 17 and 26 is what they're gonna be doing for the rest of their lives."

Chapter Thirteen: Low Dog

The streets of the neighborhood center were a paradox, alive with vibrant energy yet steeped in the undercurrent of danger that defined life in the Projects. For many, the evening's party offered a fleeting escape from the harsh realities of their world, a chance to revel in music, laughter, and community. But for Toby, the festivities were little more than a veneer, barely masking the minefield of threats that surrounded him. Toby, wise beyond his years, had already navigated more than his share of life-threatening situations. He understood all too well that in this environment, every celebration carried an edge, every moment of joy tempered by the possibility of violence.

In the shadows of this world loomed Low Dog, a name that inspired fear, respect, and fascination in equal measure. Low Dog wasn't just a man; he was a legend in the Projects, a gangster whose calculated violence and unshakable reputation had made him a figure of both awe and terror. His presence at the party that night was no accident. Misguided by lies of Dusty and Greg, driven by vengeance, Low Dog had come for Toby. The intent was clear, and the threat was imminent.

As Low Dog stalked Toby through the neighborhood, Toby's mind raced with a mix of fear and resolve. He was no stranger to danger, but this was different. Low Dog wasn't a hotheaded thug prone to reckless outbursts; he was methodical, deliberate, a predator who didn't miss his target. Toby knew that any misstep could mean not just his life, but the safety of those he cared about. Sandy, blissfully unaware of the danger, walked beside him, her cheerful chatter a stark contrast to the tension crackling in the air. Booker, still recovering from a hospital stay, leaned on Toby for support, his weakened state adding another layer of vulnerability to the group.

That night, Toby's survival hinged not just on his ability to stay calm under pressure, but on his understanding of the delicate balance between fear and bravery, aggression and restraint. The encounter with Low Dog was more than a brush with violence, it was a confrontation with the moral complexities of a world where reputation, respect, and survival were deeply intertwined.

Over time, Toby's interactions with Low Dog would evolve, shifting from moments of immediate danger to unexpected reflection. In their tense exchanges, Toby began to see the layers beneath Low Dog's fearsome exterior: a man shaped by cycles of violence and mistrust, but also one who lived by a code of principles that, in their own way, demanded respect.

The story of Toby and Low Dog is not just one of survival but of growth, understanding, and hard-won wisdom. It is a story that explores the cost of living a life driven by fear and the unexpected connections that can emerge even in the darkest corners of human experience. Through Toby's eyes, is a world where danger is ever-present, but so too is the potential for reflection, resilience, and the pursuit of a path beyond the shadows.

A Party Turned Threat

The neighborhood center was alive with music, laughter, and the mingling voices of people seeking a brief escape from the harsh realities of life in the Projects. For Toby, the party was supposed to be a reprieve, a chance to enjoy a rare moment of normalcy. Booker, recently released from the hospital and still struggling to regain full use of his arms, was leaning heavily on Toby for support. Sandy, cheerful and chatty as ever, flitted from topic to topic, oblivious to the tension that had begun to settle around them.

It wasn't long before Toby's sense of unease sharpened. Amidst the swirling crowd, he caught sight of a figure standing in the shadows: Low Dog. His presence, though silent, was as commanding as a gunshot in a quiet room. Toby knew immediately why he was there. Low Dog wasn't a man who showed up to neighborhood parties for fun or conversation, he had come for one reason, and it was written in the cold, calculating way he tracked Toby with his eyes.

Toby's heart began to pound, but outwardly, he remained calm. Showing fear was an invitation for disaster. He kept his movements measured, his face neutral, even as his mind raced through possible outcomes. Booker leaned in and whispered, "You good?" Toby nodded, though his focus never left Low Dog.

The evening wore on with an excruciating slowness. Sandy continued to chatter, completely unaware of the predator circling them. She commented on the food, the decorations, and the people, her voice a bright contrast to the tension Toby felt with every passing minute. Booker, though quiet, picked up on the danger, his own eyes flicking toward Low Dog whenever he thought Toby wasn't looking.

When it was time to leave, Toby made sure they moved as a group. The walk home was nerve-wracking, each step heavy with the knowledge that Low Dog was following them. From the opposite side of the street, Low Dog kept pace, his movements deliberate and shadowed. Toby didn't need to look to know he was there; he could feel the weight of his presence, like a hunter stalking prey.

Low Dog wasn't the type to spray bullets into a crowd or miss his target in a frenzy of violence. Toby knew that if Low Dog wanted him dead, he'd make sure it was clean and precise. That knowledge made the walk home all the more unbearable. Toby's focus wasn't on his own safety but on protecting Sandy, who had no idea the danger she was in, and Booker, whose weakened state made him vulnerable.

They finally reached their building, stepping into the faint safety of its worn hallways. Toby knew that Low Dog wouldn't risk making a move here. The risk was too high, the potential fallout too great. Still, the tension didn't leave Toby's body as he ushered Sandy and

Booker into the elevator. It wasn't until they reached the safety of their apartment that Toby allowed himself to breathe.

The encounter left Toby shaken but resolved. Low Dog's pursuit wasn't just about revenge, it was a symptom of a larger world of mistrust, misinformation, and cycles of violence. As Toby sat by the window that night, watching the street below for any sign of Low Dog, he found himself reflecting not just on the danger he had narrowly escaped but on the choices that had led both him and Low Dog to this moment.

Toby is lying awake, staring at the ceiling, knowing that the night's events were just one chapter in an ongoing struggle for survival in a world where reputation and respect could mean the difference between life and death.

The Encounter Outside the Courthouse

The air outside the courthouse was heavy with tension, a charged atmosphere born from the weight of the building's purpose. The street bustled with people, lawyers briskly walking to their next appointments, families clutching papers and whispering anxiously, and individuals lingering on the steps, waiting for their cases to be called. Amid this backdrop of legal bureaucracy, Toby found himself face-to-face with the last person he expected to see, Low Dog.

Months had passed since the night at the neighborhood center, but Toby hadn't forgotten Low Dog's calculated stalking or the palpable threat he represented. Now, standing across from him in the stark daylight, the shadows of that night seemed to resurface.

Low Dog, dressed in his usual understated but sharp style, locked eyes with Toby. There was no mistaking the intensity in his gaze, the way he commanded attention without saying a word. Toby braced himself, his heart pounding in his chest.

"You know who I am?" Low Dog asked, his voice low but steady.

Toby nodded; his response measured. "Yeah, I know. You tried to shoot me."

The honesty of Toby's words hung in the air, cutting through the ambient noise of the courthouse steps. For a moment, Low Dog looked taken aback, not by the accusation itself but by the calm way Toby had delivered it. Before Low Dog could respond, Toby continued.

"It's alright," Toby said, his tone even. "I know you were lied to. Dusty and Greg lied. I appreciate you holding back that night."

Low Dog's expression shifted, the hard edges softening ever so slightly. He tilted his head, studying Toby with a mix of curiosity and respect. "No shit," Low Dog muttered, almost to himself. "That's real."

The conversation took an unexpected turn as the tension began to dissolve. Low Dog leaned closer, his voice quieter now, more reflective. "I could tell, you know, by the way that girl was talking. Sandy, right? She didn't have a clue what was going on. I don't hurt people like that. My beef was with you."

Toby nodded, feeling a strange sense of relief. Low Dog's words confirmed what Toby had suspected: despite his reputation, Low Dog operated by a certain code. It wasn't about mindless violence or collateral damage; it was about precision and intent.

"I knew it wasn't your style," Toby replied. "And I respect that."

Low Dog gave a small, barely noticeable nod. For a man whose name was synonymous with fear and power, the moment was unexpectedly human. It wasn't forgiveness, nor was it friendship, but it was a shared understanding, a rare glimpse into the man behind the legend.

As they stood there, two men on opposite sides of a complex web of mistrust and survival, Toby found himself reflecting on the layers that made up Low Dog's persona. Beneath the fearsome exterior was someone driven by principles, even if those principles were shaped by a life of violence and mistrust.

The encounter ended with an exchange of subtle nods, an unspoken acknowledgment that the moment of danger had passed. Low Dog turned and walked away, disappearing into the crowd.

Toby remained on the steps for a while, replaying the conversation in his mind. The interaction had left him with more questions than answers. How much of Low

Dog's life was dictated by the need to uphold his reputation? How much of Toby's own life was shaped by similar pressures?

As he walked home, Toby couldn't shake the feeling that their exchange had been more than just a meeting of adversaries. It had been a rare moment of clarity in a chaotic world, a reminder that even those who seemed untouchable carried their own complexities and struggles.

Toby continues to reflect on the unexpected humanity in Low Dog's words and actions, a moment that reshaped his understanding of the man he had once feared and hated.

Low Dog's World

Toby's understanding of Low Dog's power deepened during a later encounter. It happened on a quiet evening when Toby noticed a familiar car parked at the end of the circle near his building. Low Dog stepped out, his presence as commanding as ever, but this time there was no immediate tension. He waved Toby over, gesturing for him to talk.

As Toby approached, he noticed something different in Low Dog's demeanor. There was no animosity, no sign of the predator stalking his prey. Instead, Low Dog seemed almost contemplative, his sharp eyes scanning the area as if taking in every detail.

"People talk, you know," Low Dog began, his voice calm but with an edge that demanded attention. "Everywhere I go, they come up to me. They tell me who's been saying what, who's been running their mouth."

Toby listened intently, unsure where the conversation was headed but keenly aware of the significance of Low Dog's words.

"They're all scared," Low Dog continued, a faint smile tugging at the corner of his mouth. "Even the ones who act tough. They're the first ones to come crawling, telling me who's talking shit, what they said, and when they said it."

There was a heaviness in his voice, as though he was both amused and burdened by the constant flow of information that surrounded him. "It's like they're all trying to prove something. But you know what it really is? They're scared of me. They think if they tell me enough, I won't come for them."

Toby nodded, understanding the twisted logic at play. Fear was like money in the Projects, and Low Dog had more of it than anyone. But it came at a cost, a life lived in constant awareness of whispers, betrayals, and shifting allegiances.

Low Dog turned his gaze to Toby, his expression serious now. "I'm telling you this because I like you," he said, his tone dropping to a near whisper. "Be careful who you talk to and be careful what you say about people. It always gets back to them. Always."

The words sent a chill through Toby. It wasn't just a warning, it was a lesson, one that Low Dog had clearly learned through years of navigating the treacherous waters of power and reputation.

Toby thanked him, but the encounter left him shaken. As Low Dog drove away, the weight of his advice settled heavily on Toby's mind. In a world where trust was scarce and alliances were fragile, words could be as dangerous as weapons.

In the days that followed, Toby found himself reevaluating his interactions with others. Low Dog's words echoed in his mind every time he overheard gossip or considered sharing his own thoughts. It wasn't paranoia, it was a new awareness of the delicate balance required to survive in the Projects.

Low Dog's influence on Toby wasn't one of fear alone. It was a strange mix of intimidation and respect, a reluctant mentorship that taught Toby lessons he hadn't asked for but couldn't ignore. Low Dog was a man who lived by his own code, and while that code was rooted in violence and mistrust, it also carried a certain wisdom.

Now, as Toby walks through the Projects, his eyes and ears more attuned to the whispers and currents of the world around him. Low Dog's advice had reshaped the way Toby saw his environment, teaching him that survival wasn't just about strength or cunning, it was about understanding the power of words and the weight of silence.

The Cost of Reputation

Toby sat on the worn steps outside his building, watching the familiar rhythm of life around the buildings. Children played in the distance, their laughter blending with the thumping bass of a nearby car stereo. Yet, even amidst the chaos of the neighborhood, Toby's thoughts lingered on Low Dog, the man whose name was spoken in hushed tones and whose presence commanded fear and respect.

Low Dog's influence was undeniable. People deferred to him, whispered about him, and avoided his path out of self-preservation. But as Toby reflected on their encounters, a question gnawed at him: What does it cost to live like that?

He thought about Low Dog's reputation, the weight it carried, and the sacrifices required to maintain it. Admired by some, feared by many, Low Dog's power came at a steep price. Toby realized that Low Dog didn't just live in isolation, he lived in a constant state of paranoia. Every interaction was a calculation, every person a potential threat. The same people who whispered his name with reverence also gossiped behind his back, betraying one another to stay on his good side.

Toby remembered Low Dog's warning: "Be careful who you talk to and what you say." Those words carried the weight of experience, spoken by someone who had spent his life navigating a web of deceit and mistrust. But what struck Toby most was the loneliness that came with that kind of power. Low Dog's control over others wasn't built on friendship or loyalty, it was built on fear. And fear, Toby realized, was a fragile foundation.

Despite the respect Toby felt for Low Dog's ability to command his environment, he couldn't ignore the emptiness that seemed to define his existence. Low Dog was surrounded by people, yet he was utterly alone. His reputation, for all its strength, had made him a prisoner of his own power.

Toby's reflections turned inward as he considered his own path. He had seen firsthand how quickly fear could escalate into violence, how a single misstep could lead to tragedy. Low Dog's life was a reminder of the dangers of living by the rules of the street, a life where respect was earned through intimidation and maintained through constant vigilance.

Toby realized that power without trust was a double-edged sword. While it could protect you, it could just as easily isolate you, leaving you vulnerable in ways that strength alone couldn't guard against. He thought back to the moments when Low Dog had shown humanity, his restraint at the party, his warning outside the courthouse. Those glimpses of vulnerability made Toby wonder if Low Dog himself ever questioned the path he had chosen.

Toby is standing up and looking out at the Projects, a place where every choice carried weight and every action had consequences. He resolved to live differently, to navigate the complexities of his world with integrity and measured actions. While he respected Low Dog's ability to survive, Toby knew that survival alone wasn't enough. To truly live, one had to find a way to balance power with connection, strength with compassion, and fear with understanding.

Through these reflections, Toby gained a deeper understanding of the dangers of power and the cost of a reputation built on fear. It wasn't a life he wanted, and it wasn't a legacy he wished to leave behind. For Toby, the lesson was clear: the true measure of strength lay not in domination, but in the ability to rise above the cycles of fear and violence that defined the world around him.

A Legacy in the Shadows

The news of Low Dog's death spread through the neighborhood quietly, like the passing of a storm that had lingered on the horizon for years. Liver cancer had claimed him, a disease that moved silently and without regard for the reputation he had spent a lifetime building. Toby heard the news from a neighbor, who mentioned it in passing, almost as though speaking Low Dog's name might still summon him.

For Toby, the news brought a strange mix of emotions. Relief, perhaps, that Low Dog's shadow no longer loomed over the neighborhood, but also an unexpected sadness. Their interactions had been tense, often fraught with danger, yet there had been an undeniable connection, one that left Toby reflecting on the lessons Low Dog had unknowingly imparted.

Toby sat by the window that night, staring out at the streetlights that dotted the Projects. He thought back to their final conversation, when Low Dog had warned him about the power of words and the dangers of misplaced trust. That advice, though chilling at the time, had stayed with Toby, shaping the way he navigated the world around him.

Low Dog's life was a study in contradictions. He had inspired fear, commanded respect, and maintained control, but at great personal cost. His reputation had made him powerful, but it had also isolated him, leaving him surrounded by people who feared him more than they cared for him. Yet, beneath the surface, Low Dog had revealed glimpses of humanity, a man who had spared Sandy's life, who valued honesty, and who had given Toby a piece of wisdom that was as much about survival as it was about life itself.

As Toby reflected, he realized that Low Dog's legacy wasn't just the fear he left behind but also the lessons he imparted, however unintentionally. Low Dog had shown Toby the power of discretion, the importance of reputation, and the delicate balance required to survive in a world that thrived on mistrust and violence.

Toby couldn't ignore the weight of those lessons. In the Projects, survival was a constant negotiation, between strength and restraint, between trust and caution, between action and silence. Low Dog's life, and his death, underscored the fragility of that balance. While Low Dog's reputation had kept him alive for years, it had also trapped him in a cycle of paranoia and isolation that ultimately consumed him.

Yet, Toby carried forward the wisdom Low Dog had passed on, choosing to live by a different code. He understood now that true strength wasn't just about commanding fear or respect, it was about building connections, earning trust, and navigating the complexities of life with care and integrity.

Toby stands in the quiet of his apartment, looking out at the same streets Low Dog had once ruled. He felt a deep respect for the man, not for his violence or his power, but for the lessons he had left behind. In a world that often seemed impossible to escape, Low Dog's story served as both a warning and a guide, a reminder that survival wasn't just about the battles you fought but the way you chose to live beyond them.

For Toby, Low Dog's legacy lived on, not in the shadows of fear but in the clarity of understanding. It was a legacy that Toby carried forward, not as a burden, but as a reminder of the choices that defined a life.

Chapter Fourteen: A New Leaf

Toby's time at the City Colleges of Chicago had been interrupted but not ended. He threw himself back into his studies with a drive that surprised even him.

He was finishing up the semester, and he loved it. It wasn't unusual for Toby to be there all day talking with instructors and hanging out with some of the other students.

"Toby Dunbar! Is that you?" Tammy Penn's voice rang out, her amazement cutting through the usual hum of campus life. Toby turned, his face breaking into a wide grin as he saw her. "Hey, Tammy! It's me!" he replied, laughing as he approached. Tammy Penn was a familiar face from the old neighborhood, someone who could always make Toby laugh with her quick wit and infectious humor. Her eyes sparkled with the same liveliness he remembered, and for a moment, the weight of Toby's recent past seemed to lift.

"How's Uncle Cadillac?" she asked, still laughing.

"You know Cadillac," Toby said with a grin, "he's still telling his tall tales." He leaned in slightly, lowering his voice as though sharing a secret. "He told everybody about the yard-bird and pepper grass."

Tammy doubled over with laughter, clutching her sides. "I hate to admit it, but them pigeons were good!" she said between gasps, setting both of them off in a fit of uncontrollable laughter.

Later that evening, Toby sat in his room, reflecting on his day at school. Running into Tammy had been an unexpected joy, a reminder of the simpler, sometimes absurd moments from his time in jail. He thought about Cadillac, the larger-than-life figure who always seemed to have a wild story or a crazy scheme to share. Jail had been a strange place, full of unpredictable characters, but no one left a mark quite like Cadillac.

Toby smiled to himself, almost laughing out loud as he remembered one of Cadillac's infamous tales, a mix of pure invention and just enough truth to make it plausible. Cadillac's stories had been more than entertainment; they were an escape, a way to remind everyone that even in the darkest places, there was still room for humor and humanity.

Cadillac was a big southern guy, towering over most of the inmates with an imposing frame that could easily intimidate anyone who didn't know him. He was at least twenty years older than Toby, with a weathered face that told stories of hard living and tougher times. But despite his size and the rough edges, Toby never felt threatened by him. He had a warmth that was hard to overlook, a softness that peeked through the cracks of his tough exterior. Toby knew him from the street. He was one of Tammy Penn's uncles. Toby used to love hanging out with them because they were always doing something crazy, especially the day they took him on a pigeon hunt.

"Boy, you ain't never heard a story until you've heard one from down south," he said with a booming laugh one afternoon, his thick accent rolling over the words like molasses. He leaned back in his chair, arms crossed over his chest, a smile dancing on his lips as he recounted tales of mischief and mayhem from his youth.

"Let me tell you about the time we tried to catch a raccoon for a barbecue," he began, his deep voice booming across the room, grabbing the attention of a few other inmates. "We had this old truck, and my cousin thought it would be a good idea to lure it in with a bucket of fried chicken. You can guess how that turned out!" He erupted into laughter, and soon enough, Toby found myself laughing along, even though he had no idea how the story ended. But it was one particular story that Toby would never forget, the day Cadillac decided to showcase his notorious sense of humor.

"Hey, you ever seen a foot that could clear a room faster than a fart?" Cadillac leaned in, his eyes sparkling with mischief. "I'll tell you right now, mine could do the trick." Before Toby could respond, Cadillac lifted his enormous foot and placed it squarely on the table between them both, the bare sole facing Toby. The stench hit Toby like a freight train. It was a pungent, sweaty aroma that seemed to cling to the air, wrapping around Toby like a thick fog. Toby recoiled instinctively, his face contorting in horror.

"Now, what do you think of that?" Cadillac howled, his laughter echoing through the room as the other inmates joined in. The sound was infectious, and despite his initial shock, Toby couldn't help but laugh too. It was absurd, and he realized that this was just another layer of Cadillac's twisted sense of humor.

"I wouldn't date a woman if her feet weren't as stinky as mine," he declared between fits of laughter, slapping his knee as he wiped tears from his eyes. "You gotta have standards!"

The other inmates were practically rolling on the floor, their laughter punctuating the gray walls of the jail. Toby shook his head, still chuckling, trying to imagine the kind of woman who would meet Cadillac's peculiar criteria. The whole place felt lighter for a moment, the burdens of incarceration fading into the background as we shared in the absurdity of it all.

"Guess that's why I'm single!" he added, his expression turning mock-serious as he leaned closer, eyes twinkling. "Can't find a lady who appreciates a good foot odor."

As the laughter died down, Toby looked around the room at the faces of the other inmates. In that moment, Cadillac had transformed the grim atmosphere of the jail into something almost bearable. The stories, the laughter, these were the moments that kept us going, that reminded us we were human, despite the bars that confined us.

"Just remember, Toby," Cadillac said, a grin still plastered on his face, "life's too short to take seriously. If you can't laugh at your own feet, what's the point?"

And in that moment, Toby realized that sometimes, the greatest joys come from the most unexpected places, even from a big guy with a desire for stinky feet.

An Unexpected Encounter

Toby had always enjoyed his train rides home from school. They gave him a chance to relax, to disappear into the pages of a book, and to briefly forget the chaos that often surrounded his life. On this particular day, he sat quietly in his seat, engrossed in his reading, the rhythm of the train a soothing backdrop.

When the train stopped, Toby glanced up briefly as a gay couple boarded and took the seats directly across from him. He recognized one of them instantly but didn't say anything. He had learned long ago that the best way to avoid unnecessary drama was to mind his own business.

To his surprise, the man he recognized stood up, excused himself from his partner and approached Toby with a tentative smile. "Hey, I'm sorry about busting your head with that bottle," the man said.

Toby looked up, his brow furrowing in confusion for a moment before the memory clicked. He let out a laugh. "So, Lester, you remember that?"

Lester's eyes widened. "Wait, you remember my name?"

Toby chuckled. "Yep, I remember."

Lester, clearly relieved, exhaled deeply. "Every time I see you, I think about it! I am so sorry! Your name is Toby Dunbar, right?"

"That's me," Toby replied, still laughing.

As Lester made his way back to his seat, he turned to Toby with a sheepish grin. "And that wasn't even my dog! My brother had my dog the whole time!"

Toby laughed even harder. "I was trying to tell you that it was my dog!"

The exchange caught the attention of other passengers, and soon the entire train was chuckling at the absurdity of the situation. Lester introduced Toby to his partner, and the mood on the train became light and cheerful. For a moment, it felt like the world wasn't such a bad place.

Trouble on the Train

The atmosphere shifted when two wannabe tough guys boarded the train. Their posturing and sneering were impossible to ignore, and they seemed to zero in on the cheerful energy that Lester and his partner were radiating.

"Ahh, that's so sweet," one of them mocked, his voice dripping with sarcasm.

Toby, sitting quietly, immediately felt the tension rise. He hoped they would lose interest and move on, but instead, one of them turned his attention to the couple. "So, who's the man?" he sneered, his words laced with malice.

Toby's jaw tightened. He had seen this kind of behavior before, the way bullies sought out vulnerable targets, feeding off intimidation. He didn't want trouble, especially not after everything he'd been through. But he also couldn't sit back and watch this escalate.

When one of the men moved closer to Lester and his partner, making another crude remark, Toby had enough. The last thing he wanted was to get arrested, but his temper got the better of him. He stood up, his presence immediately shifting the energy in the car.

"Y'all need to leave them alone," Toby said, his voice calm but firm.

"Or what?" one of the men shot back, stepping closer.

What happened next was quick. Toby didn't give them a chance to make the first move. In a flurry of punches and well-placed strikes, he took them both down. The so-called tough guys didn't stand a chance. By the time the train pulled into the next station, both were on the floor, groaning in pain and clutching their faces.

The Price of Action

The relief Toby felt was short-lived. When the train stopped, police officers boarded, alerted by passengers who had called about the fight. Toby explained what had happened, his frustration bubbling beneath the surface.

"They started it," he said, recounting how the men had been harassing Lester and his partner.

One officer, examining the battered faces of the two men on the floor, shook his head. "I hear you, man, but you admitted hitting them. Look at their faces. I'm sorry, but you're under arrest."

Toby's heart sank as the cuffs clicked around his wrists. He glanced at Lester, who looked stricken with guilt. "I'm sorry, Toby," Lester said softly as the officers led him away.

Toby didn't blame Lester. He had made his choice, and he would deal with the consequences. As frustrating as it was, he couldn't sit by and let bullies have their way, not then, not ever.

Later, as he was being taken to a holding cell, Toby reflected on what had happened. It wasn't the first time his sense of justice had gotten him into trouble, and it probably wouldn't be the last. But deep down, he knew he had done the right thing. Sometimes, standing up for what's right comes with a price, and Toby had always been willing to pay it.

Confrontation with Zero

Toby stepped into the large holding cell, his body tensing immediately as the cacophony of voices and footsteps reverberated off the concrete walls. He scanned the room with practiced caution, his eyes darting across faces, some familiar, others unfamiliar. Then, cutting through the noise, he heard a voice that froze him in his tracks.

"Hey Toby!" It was Zero. If there was ever a person Toby despised with every fiber of his being, it was Zero. The sight of him made Toby's stomach churn, his hands instinctively curling into fists. Zero wasn't just a man from his past; he was a living reminder of one of the most painful moments in Toby's life, the death of Rick.

Toby's gaze locked onto Zero's, his eyes burning with unspoken rage. Memories of Rick surged to the forefront of his mind, unrelenting and raw. He remembered the arguments they used to have, the way Rick had insisted that Zero's drug sales in the building across from theirs were raking in $15,000 a day. Toby had argued fiercely, calling it impossible.

"How could families living in low-income apartments generate that much money?" Toby had countered, running the numbers in his head. Seven buildings, fifteen stories each, ten apartments per floor, it just didn't add up.

But Rick had been right. Toby realized too late that the money didn't come from the residents of the Projects. Most of it came from outsiders, drawn by the promise of a quick high. Rick had known the truth because he had become part of that world, a victim of the very drugs they had sworn to avoid.

The memory of Rick lying dead in front of him flashed in Toby's mind. It had been more than he could bear. Rick, his lifelong friend, the one who had been there for him countless times, was gone. Toby remembered how his knees had buckled as he cried in disbelief, his body wracked with pain and anger.

Underneath his grief had been a simmering fury, anger at Rick for falling victim to drugs and for breaking their most important rule: stay away from the poison that consumed their enemies. But Toby's anger extended to himself as well. He had failed to push Rick toward a better path, failed to save him from the darkness. The guilt still lingered, a heavy weight that never truly lifted.

The thing that haunted Toby the most was knowing how Zero and his crew had killed Rick. They hadn't just shot him; they had toyed with him, holding him down and taunting him before delivering the fatal blow. Zero had known Rick was unarmed, he'd traded his pistols for drugs earlier that day.

Toby's rage burned hotter as he remembered the details. Zero and his goons had driven by first, firing shots that struck Rick in the leg and side. Rick had tried to run, limping and staggering across the row of apartments near Mr. Davis's place, but he hadn't stood a chance.

Now, standing just feet away from Zero, Toby forced himself to remain calm. He wouldn't let Zero see how much anger still boiled beneath the surface.

"Oh yeah, remember Jake?" Zero asked casually, breaking the tense silence.

Toby didn't respond, his expression cold and unreadable.

"Well, he got shot," Zero continued, watching for a reaction.

"Really?" Toby replied flatly, his tone dripping with indifference.

Zero smiled faintly, his voice taking on a mocking edge. "You didn't have anything to do with it, did you?"

Still, Toby said nothing. Instead, he held Zero's gaze, his silence more powerful than any words could have been. Slowly, deliberately, Toby raised his middle finger and scratched an old scar above his eyebrow, a reminder of a fight he had survived. Then, without breaking eye contact, he lowered his hand and scratched the old scar below his bottom lip.

The message was clear. Toby wasn't the same boy Zero had known. He was a man now, forged by pain, loss, and survival.

Zero's smile faded slightly as the realization dawned on him. "Not the same little Toby Dunbar, huh?" he muttered, his tone quieter now.

For the first time, Zero seemed to understand that Toby was no longer someone he could dismiss or toy with. There was a strength in Toby's silence, a calmness that demanded respect.

Zero nodded slowly, acknowledging the shift in their dynamic. He might have once seen Toby as an easy target, but now he saw him as a man who had faced the fire and emerged unbroken. The balance of power had shifted, and both men knew it.

As Zero turned and walked away, Toby exhaled, his body still tense but his resolve stronger than ever. This wasn't just a confrontation, it was a reminder of how far he'd come and how much he'd endured. Zero's presence would always remind him of Rick, but it also reminded him of the promise he had made to himself: to survive, to grow, and to never let anyone take away his strength again.

Toby was released from the lock-up the next morning.

Chapter Fifteen: A Return to Familiar Doors

The knock on Sandy's door felt heavier than usual, as if Toby's guilt and frustration were embedded in the sound. When Sandy opened the door, her face immediately registered concern. "Oh no! Again, Toby? What happened?" she asked, her voice a mix of worry and disappointment.

Toby sighed, his shoulders slumping as if the weight of her question were too much to bear. "I know. I'm sorry, Sandy, but they had it coming," he replied, his voice low and apologetic. He avoided her eyes, knowing the sight of his battered face only reinforced Mrs. May's warnings.

From inside the house, Mrs. May's voice cut through the moment like a blade. "I told you he was nothing but trouble!" she shouted, her frustration spilling over. Toby raised his hand in an awkward wave. "Hello, Mrs. May!" he called out, trying to inject a bit of humor into the tense situation.

"Ahh, shut up talking to me, boy!" Mrs. May snapped, her tone sharp and unrelenting.

Sandy turned to her mother, her own frustration evident. "Mama, you don't have to be like that," she said, her voice firm but respectful. She turned back to Toby, her expression softening. "I'm sorry, Toby," she said quietly.

Toby shook his head and looked down; his hands shoved into his pockets. "Don't feel bad about that," he muttered. "She's right. Try to stop by later." With that, he turned and walked away, his mind swirling with thoughts he couldn't quite silence.

Reflections on a Cycle of Violence

Mrs. May's words lingered in Toby's mind as he walked, each step feeling heavier than the last. She's right, he thought to himself. I am trouble. It wasn't the first time he'd heard those words, and he doubted it would be the last. But this time, they carried a weight that went beyond Mrs. May's sharp tone. They forced him to confront a question he had been avoiding for years: was violence simply a part of who he was?

He thought about the men he'd met in jail, men who had spent so much time locked up that they struggled to adapt to life on the outside. Milton had a term for it: institutionalized. Toby had scoffed at the idea before, but now it felt uncomfortably close to home. He hadn't been in jail long compared to most, but the habits, the survival instincts, the reflexes, they were all still there, shaping his every move.

Toby contrasted his life with the stories his classmates at the City Colleges told. Their worries were about grades, part-time jobs, and dating, not survival, not threats of violence around every corner. The gap between their world and his felt insurmountable. For them, the level of violence Toby had grown used to was unfathomable, something that only happened in movies or the evening news. For him, it was a daily reality.

Maybe Milton was right. Maybe living in the Projects, in an environment where tension simmered just beneath the surface, had its own kind of institutionalizing effect. The idea gnawed at Toby. Is it fair to blame the Projects? he wondered. Or is it just me? Am I the problem?

The deeper Toby dug into his thoughts, the more he realized how entangled his life was with violence. It seemed like there was always something, a fight, a threat, a confrontation. Even when he tried to walk away, trouble found him. Was it the world he lived in, or was it something inside him, something he couldn't escape no matter how hard he tried?

As Toby made his way back to his apartment, Mrs. May's voice echoed in his mind. I told you he was nothing but trouble! He clenched his fists, not out of anger, but out of frustration with himself. He didn't want to be trouble. He didn't want Sandy to see him as just another lost cause. But as much as he tried to change, the cycle always seemed to pull him back in.

Toby sighed deeply, staring at the cracked pavement beneath his feet. Is it ever going to end? he thought. The question hung in the air, unanswered, as he disappeared into the night, carrying the weight of a past he couldn't escape and a future he couldn't yet see.

Bad News

The sound of the telephone ringing abruptly pulled Toby from his thoughts. "Ring... ring... ring..."

"Hey Toby, it's for you!" one of his younger brothers yelled. "It's Milton!"

Toby rushed to the phone; his excitement palpable. "Hey Milton!"

But the voice on the other end wasn't the Milton he knew. There was something different, strained, subdued. "Hey Toby, how's it going out there? How's school?" Milton asked, his tone flat.

Before Toby could answer, another voice cut through the line. Cold. Familiar. "You're done. Hang up the phone, Milton."

Toby's blood ran cold as the call abruptly ended with a sharp click. It was Picasso. They had Milton.

The next morning, Toby was still shaken when Sandy came rushing into the apartment, her breath labored. "Toby, Dusty and Greg were in the lobby looking for you!" she said, her voice trembling.

Toby's stomach knotted. Dusty and Greg weren't just nuisances, they were harbingers of trouble. "What do they want?" he asked, though he already knew the answer wasn't good. Sandy tried to reassure him, but Toby could only nod, forcing himself to stay calm. "It's okay," he said quietly, though his mind was anything but.

Two days later, as if the situation couldn't worsen, a friend knocked on Toby's door, holding a letter in his hand. "Hey man, this was on the lobby floor. You need to see it."

The words on the page blurred as Toby read, his mind struggling to process the shock. The letter mentioned a grand jury indictment and, more devastatingly, stated that Toby had to return to jail. His heart sank. Freedom, so fleeting, seemed to slip through his fingers once again.

Toby sat down, gripping the letter tightly. The events of the past few days, Picasso's voice on the phone, Dusty and Greg's sudden appearance, and now this letter, felt like a noose tightening around him. The past he thought he had left behind was clawing its way back into his life, and this time, it felt like it wouldn't let go without a fight.

Made in the USA
Monee, IL
13 March 2025

7d5c1e3f-8d29-405f-8523-fddabdb8cf71R01